CRUEL PROMISE

DOMINIQUE & KASEY

DEVILS OF SUN VALLEY
BOOK 4

DANIELA ROMERO

COFFEE
and
CHARACTERS

BEFORE YOU BEGIN

ONE
DOMINIQUE

If there is one commandment in life every man should honor, it's *thou shall not fuck your best friend's baby sister*. Problem is, I broke that one already and I continue to fucking break it with zero end in sight.

I knew screwing Kasey Henderson would earn me a one-way ticket to hell. Honest to god, I was very well aware of what a horrible and fucked up idea getting involved with her was. There is a reason I've denied myself all these years.

The path leading to her was lit up with neon caution signs and "Stop! Turn back!" warnings so damn big and bright they were impossible to ignore. But like the fool my father often proclaims me to be, I turned a blind eye to every single one of them.

It's easy to think you have shit under control when the years roll by without incident. When you get in the habit of ignoring your wants. Your fucking needs. You assume you have your shit together. That you can walk away without a single problem.

I grew complacent and it is biting me in the ass.

Kasey Henderson has always drawn my attention. And not always in a good way. At first, she was impossible to ignore simply because that girl can get under my skin in a way no one else could.

She always has a smartass comment or some pissy comeback for everything I say. It drives me insane. It's as if she takes pride in aggravating me.

I tried to banish her to the category of annoying little sister because for years that's all she was to me. My friend's annoying as shit baby sister. But as the years rolled by, something about the way I looked at her changed.

Kasey still goes out of her way to infuriate me but she's not that scrawny kid she once was. She blossomed in high school and despite her shit personality, there's a lot more for a man to appreciate now. Things I've spent the last five years or better forcing myself to ignore.

It was easy to push thoughts of how good she looked or how great I imagined she would taste from my mind after I graduated. There were fewer opportunities for our paths to cross and you know how the saying goes. *Out of sight. Out of mind.*

I moved on to Suncrest U while Kasey had three years left to complete at Sun Valley High. The four-year age difference between us, and knowing she was still in high school was more reason to ignore any attraction I might have to her. To ignore *her* all together.

Aaron would kill me if I hurt his sister which, let's be honest, is exactly what I'd do. I'm not a relationship sort of guy. Something the women around me are unable to accept but that's their problem. Not mine.

I've spent too long working my ass off in football to throw it away by getting distracted by some chick. And knowing that, plus taking her age and the fact that she's my best friend's kid sister into consideration, it was easy to convince myself that nothing could ever go down between us.

But those excuses aren't reason enough to continue keeping me away. It's a big fucking problem.

Kasey is eighteen now. No longer a kid. She's doing that running start program that lets her take college courses as a high school senior.

She's at my school. Living right on campus at the Kappa Mu sorority house. A house that is only a few blocks away from my place. It was bad enough trying to avoid her in our friend group.

Worse when we registered at Suncrest U and started going to the same school.

But the real problem I'm having now, is that Kasey is still in my bed. And she's been in my bed, or I've been in hers, damn near every night for two weeks.

Ever since her mom died.

Scrubbing a hand over my face, I look at her sleeping form, huddled beneath the blankets with just her curly blond head poking out. Having her here, in my space, it shouldn't bring a smile to my face but it does. Something about her being here soothes something inside of me. It quiets all the noise. The incessant voices telling me what to do, or how to act. What my future has to be versus what I want it to be.

All of that shit falls away when she's here. But that doesn't make what we're doing right. It's wrong. Very, very wrong.

How the fuck did I let things get this far?

With a sigh, I rub the back of my neck. I'm torn between spreading her thighs and sinking into her needy center, or taking a cold ass shower until I can get my head on straight.

Fuck. I need to get her out of my bed.

It's been two weeks. That's how much time has passed since she came to me, begging for me to take away her pain. To fuck her until she couldn't think or feel. Until it no longer hurt to breathe.

She wanted to forget about her life and about her mom dying. And I could do that. I could offer her some semblance of relief. But this was supposed to be a temporary thing. A way to bury her grief until she was ready to face it.

I don't know what it is anymore.

I thought giving in and fucking her would get her out of my system. Make these fucking cravings for her go away. But all it's done is make me want her more. Kasey is a drug I desperately need to quit.

There is no future of mine in which she can be anything more to me than Aaron's little sister, whether I want her to be or not.

And for the record, I don't.

I can admit to liking having her around. The sex is great and when I'm inside her, the only words coming out of her mouth are *yes, more,* and *please.* Words I don't hear out of that smart mouth of her very often.

But great sex doesn't change who we are. Or the fact that we don't get along. At our best, we tolerate one another. At our worst, we're at each other's throats. No matter how you spin this, what we're doing right now is a recipe for disaster so why the hell haven't I put an end to it?

In some weird and messed up way, Kasey needs me. And not as a shoulder to cry on or someone to confide in.

If it was that easy, I'd be her friend. Or at least, I'd try to be. Hell, I actually did try, and it blew up in my face.

I tried to pump the brakes after the first few times we slept together. I pulled back and gave her some space. Space I assumed she needed, you know, to really grieve her mom and get her head on straight.

I still checked in on her, of course. I'm not a monster. I made sure she wasn't alone. Had Allie and Bibiana calling her or dropping by each day. And I reminded my own sister, Monique, to check in on her, too. Kasey had all of the support she could need.

But if I thought backing off was doing her some kind of favor, I was wrong.

Instead of leaning on her friends, she spent her free time getting wasted and starting fights with random ass people who looked at her funny.

It's like what little common sense she had in that pretty little head of hers flew right out the fucking window. And all I could think was it was my fucking fault.

Seeing a shiner on her face for the first time made me fucking murderous, and there wasn't a damn thing I could do about it. Not when it came from another chick after Kasey threw the first freaking punch. I still don't know what the hell started it. I don't think Kasey does either.

She turned her grief into anger and lashed out at anyone unlucky enough to cross her path. She almost got herself kicked out of her sorority—not that I would have cared about that one. In fact, I almost wish she did. Maybe then she'd accept Aaron's offer and move into our guest room, where I could keep an eye on her. But it's like she needed a new outlet once I took sex off the table and Kasey was spiraling.

I held back as long as I could but Aaron was gone, dealing with his mother's remains, and she was ignoring everyone else. What was I supposed to do?

The only way I knew how to fix it was to give her what she wanted. What she outright begged me for. And the fact that she begged me for anything at all is crazy to think about because Kasey hates me. But she sure as hell enjoys fucking me.

When her mom first died, she barely talked or ate. She was this empty shell of herself and sex... it helps. It did then, and it still does now. And if my choices are between watching her waste away, standing by as she spirals, or fucking her to the point of exhaustion so she can sleep and eat and fucking function, is it much of a choice at all?

My phone vibrates in my pocket, and I hastily pull it out to see Aaron's name flash across the screen.

Hitting accept, I bring it to my ear and try to put thoughts of Kasey aside.

"Hey man. Everything good?" I know it isn't. How could it be? His mom died, and he had to fly across the country to claim her body, jumping through endless hoops without getting time to deal with his own grief because taking a dead body across state lines comes with bullshit rules and red tape.

I'm worried about my best friend. Much like his sister, he has a rough time with real life shit like this. He doesn't know how to process it and when shit hits the fan for Aaron, things usually go sideways. His former method of coping is to use drugs. An option he no longer has access to.

In high school, it started with weed. Then for a while he turned to pills. And when that didn't cut it, he went off the deep end and started messing around with coke.

Getting into drugs wasn't entirely his fault. There were outside factors at play but none of them are present now and I won't let him get hooked on that shit again.

Aaron's been clean for two years, but there's this voice in the back of my mind telling me it's only a matter of time. Once an addict, always an addict. I have to be vigilant. Look for any signs that he might be about to dive off the deep end again.

Aaron's drawn-out sigh confirms my earlier thought that no, everything is not good, but he tries to pretend it is and since I'm not there with him and can't do shit about it right now, I let the lie slide. But I'll need to get a better read on him when gets back to Sun Valley.

"Yeah. The funeral home got around to having her cremated. Fucking finally," He grumbles. "I can fly back first thing tomorrow if that's not too soon."

"Not at all," I say, careful to keep my voice down. "I'll get the flight arranged. It'll be good to have you back." I glance to see that she's still asleep. "Good for Kasey, too."

I'm not close with my own sister. We went to different high schools and had vastly different lives. I rejected damn near everything my parents wanted for me growing up while Monique was the one who always fell in line.

It made things strained between us at times. But, I've always made it a point to look out for her. To be there whenever she needs me and I know Aaron tries to do the same for Kasey. But he hasn't been able to this time around.

They should have been able to lean on one another, but with all the arrangements that've needed to be made, there's been no time. Maybe once he gets back, Kasey will sort herself out and she won't need me anymore.

The thought makes my brows pull together and a tight feeling takes root in my chest but I ignore it when Aaron releases another sigh. I can tell without needing to see him that he's pacing whatever hotel room he's staying in, his nerves likely frayed.

"How is she doing?"

My mouth twists into a grimace and I consider how best to answer that question. Kasey's not okay. Not by a long shot. But neither is Aaron.

Telling him how messed up his baby sister is when he's thousands of miles away unable to do a damn thing about it, isn't going to do anything but add stress to an already stressful situation. And I'm not looking to make matters worse.

"As good as can be expected," I tell him, which isn't a lie. "She's sleeping but... do you want me to wake her so you two can talk?"

Shit. Too late, I realize I fucked up and admitted to having her here, in my bed. Or, *not* in my bed. She's stayed in our guestroom a handful of times before so he might assume that's where she is now. Okay. That could work. But what's my excuse for her being here? It's one thing for her to stay over when Aaron is here but there's no reason for Kasey to hang around when only I'm in residence. Shit.

Thankfully Aaron's too much in his own head to notice my mistake. "No," he spits out quickly before exhaling a heavy breath. "Sorry. That came out wrong. But, let her sleep. I'm sure she needs it"

I grunt just as Kasey stirs, a soft sigh escaping her that I pray Aaron doesn't hear.

She rolls over in bed, her eyelashes fluttering before she opens her eyes and scans the room. Catching sight of me, she meets my gaze and without needing to say a word, the air thickens between us.

The blanket beneath her shifts to expose the tops of her creamy breasts and I have to fight to keep myself rooted in place.

I can't touch her while I'm on the phone with her brother. But that doesn't stop me from looking my fill and checking her out. I'm only human after all.

Kasey sees my eyes drop to her chest before returning to her face and she gives me a heated look, one filled with filthy promise.

She pushes up on her elbows, letting the covers fall further down until the pink tips of her nipples are on display. *Shit.*

With heavy lids, she cups one hand over her breast and rolls one tight bud between her fingers, teasing me with the sight of her as she plays with herself.

My cock jerks in my gym shorts and I hiss out a breath. Slicing my hand through the air, I give her a silent order to cut that shit out. One she happily ignores.

Kasey tilts her head and a mischievous glint lights up her baby blues before she ever so fucking slowly draws the blanket back, exposing inch after inch of bare, naked skin.

"Fuck me," I groan.

"What?" Aaron asks and I jerk away from my phone only to curse myself and press it back to my ear. I give Kasey an admonishing look, one she pretends not to see as she continues to toy with her tits. It's a silent invitation I wish I could accept.

Grinding my teeth together, I turn my back on her so I can finish my call with Aaron before I close the distance between us and cross yet another line—like finger fucking my best friend's sister while I'm on the goddamn phone with him. *Christ.* What is wrong with me?

"Sorry. Got a text about practice," I lie. "Do you want me to pick you up from the airport?" I block out the sound of Kasey shifting her weight on the mattress behind me and wait for his response, but my body is tight with anticipation, my dick already hard and eager for the girl laying only a few feet away from me.

"Nah. I'll catch a ride share. Just wanted to give you a head's up that I'll be back tomorrow."

"Got it. I'll let Kasey know once she's up."

"Thanks, man." He ends the calls and before I've even returned my phone to my pocket, small arms wrap around me from behind and boldly slide beneath my shirt.

Closing my eyes, I tilt my head to the sky, and pray for the strength to resist her, knowing I won't find it. It's not supposed to be like this.

One minute we're fighting and the next we're fucking. Rinse and repeat. Neither one of us able to get enough of the other. It's not healthy. She's using sex to avoid grieving. Hell, she's using me and I should not be as cool with that as I am.

"Hi." She presses her lips to my back, hands flexing possessively against my abdomen. "Tired?"

I look over my shoulder to see a stark naked Kasey pressed up against me, giving me a terrific view of the tops of her breasts and the swell of her perfect ass.

Could she have thrown on a shirt? Of course not. She's... I shake my head. Kasey is something else. Comfortable in her own skin. Confident in her sexuality. It shouldn't surprise me. She's always known who she is and what she wants, and to hell with what anyone else thinks about it.

Despite her inexperience, Kasey is fully aware of the effect she has on me, a point she makes clear when one of her small hands dips low to brush over the hard-on I'm sporting in my gym shorts.

Biting back a groan, I hang my head and struggle to steady my breath.

Emboldened by my reaction, Kasey cups me over the fabric of my shorts, squeezing my length with her delicate fingers as she works me up and down. *Fuuuuck.*

"Hmm?"

Does she expect me to answer? I can hardly think let alone form coherent words when she's naked and touching me like this.

I shake my head and turn to face her. Wrapping my arms around her lower back, I tug her in close, smashing her breasts to my chest. Kasey's lips part on a gasp and I lean forward biting at her full bottom lip. She jerks back at the sting but my grip on her keeps her in place.

"No. I'm not tired." Not anymore.

I had to leave early this morning. Coach has me coming in for physical therapy at five am followed by weight training before my classes start while my shoulder recovers.

Between the early mornings, practice, and the marathon of sex with Kasey, I've been lucky to grab four or five hours of sleep each night, but seeing her like this and feeling her body pressed into mine pushes thoughts of sleep to the furthest recesses of my mind.

"Why? Did you miss me?" I quirk a brow enjoying the irritation that flashes across her face.

"Definitely not." She snaps.

"Oh really?"

Her expressions turns haughty. "Really."

Dipping my head, I capture her lips, taking my time to taste and explore her mouth. She hums in approval, delicate hands wrapping around my neck as she lifts up on the tips of her toes to deepen the kiss but Kasey is not the one in control right now.

To hell if she thinks I'll be the one to submit and relinquish the reins.

"So that must be why you're desperately trying to climb me like a tree. Because you didn't miss me."

Kasey pushes against my chest and this time, I release her.

"Fuck you, Dom."

I snort. "Baby girl. What have I been doing?"

Nostrils flaring she folds her arms over her chest. She wants to tell me off but she wants me to fuck her more, which reminds me, "Aaron gets back tomorrow."

I'm not telling her anything she doesn't already know. She heard enough of our conversation to realize we're running out of time. We can't keep sneaking around like this. It's one thing with him gone, but I live with the guy. If we keep doing what we're doing, he's bound to find out about it and we both agreed at the start of all of this that that could never happen.

There are too many years of friendship there to just throw it down the drain.

Kasey rocks back on her heels and raises her gaze to mine, scowling at me through a thick veil of blond lashes. "Your point?" She isn't fooling anyone with that tone.

She's just as concerned about her brother finding out about us as I am.

"And that means you can't lie naked in my bed all day anymore." No matter how much I enjoy having her in it. I don't like people in my space. Whenever I hooked up with a chick before, I made it a point to go back to their place instead of mine so I could avoid the awkward moment post orgasm when you hand the girl her clothes and offer to call her a ride. This way, I leave when I'm done and I come off as less of an asshole when I tell them I have early practice, otherwise I'd stay.

Complete and utter bullshit but it makes chicks feel better.

When it comes to Kasey though, none of that seems to happen. She comes to my place more than I ever go to hers. And after we both find our release, I wind up pinning her close to my chest and demanding that she stay.

I'd be a dick if I didn't, right? She's sleeping with me to help with her grief. Kicking her out of my bed would be in bad taste. I can be cruel. But I'm not *that* cruel.

Jutting out her bottom lip, Kasey lifts one shoulder in a half-hearted shrug. "Fine. I'll lay naked in my bed all day. We can..." she waves a hand in the air, "do *this,* over there."

"Screw?" I ask. "You're suggesting we screw back at your place?" Pretty sure I heard that wrong.

Her cheeks turn a pretty shade of pink. "Yeah. Why not?"

Closing my eyes, I count to ten, praying for strength I do not have because while it is a terrible idea—and one sure to blow up in our faces—it could be worse. I think. But has she thought this through? The last time we hooked up at her place we were nearly caught.

"Or," I suggest. "You could stop hiding and deal with your shit." I move to tuck a blond curl behind her ear, but she jerks away from me, meeting my words with a fierce glower.

"I'm not hiding," she snaps. "I like sex. There's nothing wrong with that."

She pulls away from me and I curl my hands into fists to keep myself from grabbing for her again.

"I never said there was anything wrong with it." I like sex just as much as the next guy and I just so happen to like it with Kasey Henderson a little more.

"Then what is your issue? I thought we had a deal?" Her nostrils flare.

I've pissed her off, but she isn't thinking rationally about this right now and I'm trying real fucking hard not to be the selfish asshole here.

"You just suggested we move this to your place."

"And?" She stomps across the room, retrieving her clothes from the other day and I watch with regret as she angrily tugs them on, shoving her legs into her jeans and throwing her shirt on without bothering to put her bra on first. Instead, she fists the material in her hands and folds her arms over her chest once more but she doesn't move to leave.

It's almost like she's daring me to object. Maybe even to ask her to stay. But I'm not the kind of guy to beg anyone to stick around. If she wants to storm out of here in a huff, I won't stop her. And I sure as shit won't chase after her.

"You didn't want me at the Kappa Mu house before," I remind her.

Hell, whenever I came around, she made it her mission to chase me away and I get it. I may not have liked it. But I understood her reasons.

Kasey doesn't like unwanted attention, and being the quarterback for Suncrest U comes with my fair share of it. Which is why her little suggestion won't work. What is she even thinking? That we can somehow keep fucking and her sorority sisters won't say anything to anyone about it if we get caught? All it takes is one slip up. One mistake And what we're doing will get to Aaron and the rest of our friend group. It's a bad idea.

"I wasn't having sex with you before," she snaps.

"And as soon as you were, we almost got caught."

Tears spring to her eyes. Shit. This conversation isn't going the way I expected.

"Are you just done?" There's an emotion in her voice I can't name, but it sounds oddly ... vulnerable. I don't like the way that question sounds coming from her lips. And I sure as hell don't like the way she's attempting to mask her face, wiping her expression clean as though she can hide from me. Fuck that.

If not for the shine in her eyes, I wouldn't know how upsetting the idea of stopping is to her.

But before I can say anything, she continues not slowing down to so much as take a breath.

"If you're over it, then fine. But have the balls to say it. Don't make excuses about Aaron coming home. You slept with me before he left, too, in case you forgot. But it's fine. You're ready to move on. Message received."

No. It is not fucking fine. And what message? I'm not giving her any sort of fucking message. I'm trying to have a goddamn conversation.

Moving closer, I work to eliminate the distance between us, but Kasey retreats, taking one step after the other away from me. I'm tempted to growl at her—growl, like a goddamn animal. Why is she running from me? Her back meets the wall, leaving her nowhere to go and I give her a hard look.

Crowding her against my bedroom wall, I brace my arms on either side of her, caging her in. "Kasey—" She refuses to look at me.

Gaze averted, her low lip trembles before she bites it, stilling the motion. Ice fills my veins. Is she going to cry? *Hell no.* I cannot deal with waterworks right now.

Pressing my thumb beneath her chin, I force her face up and wait until she gives in and lifts her eyes to mine.

"I never said I was done," I tell her, dipping my voice low.

Some of the tension falls from her shoulders but not all of it.

"Then what are you saying, Dom?"

Hell if I know. There is no easy answer here. We should not be fucking. That much is obvious. But that doesn't mean I want to stop fucking. Christ. Why does this have to be so complicated? "I'm not saying anything, but—"

"Aaron can't find out," she finishes for me and I nod, grateful that at least when it comes to her brother, we're on the same page. "Fine. We'll make sure he doesn't find out."

She makes it sound easy, like sleeping together behind his back is some walk in the fucking park, but keeping this secret is already one of the hardest things I've had to do. And I don't relish the idea of continuing to do it.

TWO
KASEY

Dom's conscience is getting the best of him. *Surprise. Surprise.* Who knew the asshole even had one?

As soon as I realized my brother was on the phone with him, I knew it was guilt that I'd spotted written all over Dom's face. Worry and guilt and maybe even a little fear. For someone usually so good at masking their emotions, his were right there for once. Clear as day.

I don't know what he's so afraid of. Aaron isn't going to find out about... whatever *this* between us, even is. If he'd take a step back and look at the whole picture, he'd see that keeping things under wraps isn't some monumental feat. But Dom is trying to balance being both a friend and a fuck buddy, and it'd be better for the both of us if he just gave it a rest.

I might be selfish but this isn't one sided. Dominique enjoys fucking me as much as I like being fucked by him. He just needs a reminder of that and I'm happy to give it to him if it gets me what I want.

Leaning forward, I tilt my face up toward him. With Dominique towering over me the way he is, it puts us closer despite the considerable height difference, but not close enough unless he decides to play ball and dips down just a bit further.

Well, fuck. I need him to make the dip.

"He doesn't have to find out," I whisper before running my hands up the hard planes of Dominique's chest. "We'll be careful."

His muscles flex beneath my hands. I knew Dom was in shape. Hard not to be when you're a division one athlete and the star quarterback for Suncrest U. But I don't think I ever realized just how incredible his body was until I got up close and personal with him, able to peel back all those pesky layers of clothes hiding the dark ropes of corded muscle that cover him from head to toe.

He says nothing in response to my statement, but neither does he pull away. I can work with that. Wrapping my hands around the back of his neck, I arch my back until my body presses into his. This would work better if I was still naked. Probably should have thought of that before, but, oh well. It'll have to do.

Dominique's throat contracts, his Adam's apple bobbing, as his eyes flood with desire.

Hook.

I lean in, trailing the column of his throat with wet, open mouth kisses.

He shudders beneath my touch.

Line.

"You're not done." I murmur against his flesh, reminding him of his earlier statement.

He bites out a curse and closes the few inches between us, pressing his forehead to mine. His warm breath fans over my face as he says, "No. I'm not done with you yet, baby girl."

And sinker.

The endearment has the corners of my mouth kicking up into a smile. I used to hate when he called me things like that. Especially Baby Henderson. Like being Aaron's little sister is the only title I'm worthy of. But hearing him call me baby girl, there's just something about the way he says it that makes liquid heat pool in my belly.

Dominique dips his head and captures my lips with his own, giving me the kiss I'd wordlessly asked for.

I moan into his mouth, fingers kneading into the back of his neck when he bends low, grabbing me by the backs of my thighs as though I weigh nothing before hoisting me into his arms. On instinct, I wrap my legs around his waist, keeping my mouth fused with his as he blindly carries me to his still rumpled bed.

When his shins meet the bed frame, he pauses while continuing to devour my mouth. Our teeth clash together but neither one of us seems to care. Dominique's lips are firm and demanding as he lays siege to my mouth, taking control of the kiss and forcing me into submission.

Most days I'd be inclined to fight him on it but today, I relinquish my control with little protest.

Intent on forgetting the world and sinking into the feel of his touch.

Dom's fingers dig into my ass and I melt further into his embrace before his hold shifts on my body. He moves his hands to my hips and, with a firm grip, he shoves me away from him, throwing me onto the mattress.

I gasp, the air whooshing out of my lungs on impact, and for a split second, I'm taken with how rough he is. But the thought leaves my head almost as soon as it enters my mind when he tears his shirt over his head and shoves down both his gym shorts and briefs, leaving himself deliciously naked before me and making me breathless for an entirely new reason.

His cock juts out between us, fully erect and demanding attention. I never thought dicks were anything special. A weird-looking body part that makes you feel good assuming the guy knows what to do with it. Which can be a toss up from what I've heard.

But Dominique knows what to do with his and there is nothing weird about it. I was hesitant at first—because holy hell is he huge—but I've really developed a thing for

Dominique's dick, and I feel zero shame lying here and admiring it.

His dick is long and thick, wrapped in dark brown skin, the blunt head a few shades lighter than the rest of him.

I stare shamelessly as he wraps his hand around his erection, stroking himself with quick, firm strokes. His eyes burn as he presses one knee to the mattress between my legs, his intentions abundantly clear.

A drop of pre-cum leaks from his tip and I lick my lips, mouth watering at the remembered taste and feel of it, but Dominique doesn't look like he's in the mood for much foreplay. His jaw is clenched, nostrils flared. I take him in, soaking in his cruel, masculine beauty.

Without a word, he releases himself and hooks his fingers into my still unbuttoned jeans before tearing them down my legs, taking my panties along with them.

I move to sit up so I can help tug off my shirt, but a hand pressed to the center of my chest stops me. Dominique shoves me flat back on the bed, eyes locking with mine, almost daring me to look away.

Grabbing my knees, he forces my legs wide, exposing my pussy to his hungry gaze. I shiver underneath the intensity of his stare, my legs clenching together, but his grip only tightens, keeping me in place.

"Tell me what you need." It's not a question. It's a demand.

"You." I'm panting now, desperate for him to fuck me and not at all ashamed to admit it, but he just stands there, looking his fill as I lie beneath him.

"Keep your legs open for me. Understand?"

I do as instructed and am rewarded when he swipes two thick fingers through my folds. A moan slips past my lips before he withdraws his touch, bringing his fingers to his mouth, and mine drops open at the site of what he does next.

Dominique sucks both fingers into his mouth, licking the evidence of my desire clean from his fingertips before murmuring a soft groan, eyes closed like I am the best thing he has ever tasted.

My pussy clenches, more proof of how turned on I am now leaking between my thighs. *Fuck.* Why is that so hot? It's obscene yet I'm completely turned on by the action.

My heart races and eager anticipation thrums through me as I wait to see what he'll do next. I need him to touch me. Okay, I need him to do a lot more than that, but you get the idea. What I do not need though, is for him to talk. Which is what he decides to do right now.

"If we keep doing this, I'm setting new rules," he tells me.

A frown carves itself into my face. "What new rules?" We already made rules. Keep it casual. Don't catch feelings. No fucking anyone else because—gross. And Aaron can never find out. What more does he want? And more, why the hell is he bringing this up now when I am half naked and here for the taking?

Dominique returns his fingers between my thighs, running them back and forth along my slit without penetrating me.

Holy ...

... yes...

More...

"So fucking wet. This all for me?" With his other hand, he shoves my shirt up, exposing my breasts before leaning down to capture one in his mouth, teeth biting down on my nipple right as he slides his fingers higher to find my clit.

The sharp stab of pain shoots an arrow of heat straight to my center, taking me higher and higher as Dom circles my clit with quick, confident strokes.

My hips thrust forward, but a hand on the inside of my thigh presses me back, preventing me from chasing his touch.

"Rule number one," he says, still circling my clit.

Really? We're back to this? I thought after the last comment that he would drop it.

"You go back to class."

I open my mouth to reject the idea when he moves his hand and thrusts two thick fingers into my pussy. I gasp, clenching around him and he continues. "Rule number two. You respond to my calls. All of them. I don't give a shit if you're busy or it's the middle of the night. If I call, you fucking answer."

Jesus Christ. Demanding much? I've ignored him—at most—maybe three times since this thing between us started. Okay, more like five. But who cares? All he wanted was to check up on me. I'm eighteen years old and Dominique Price is not my keeper.

He thrusts his fingers in and out, making it hard to concentrate as my body coils tight, fingers fisting into the sheets at my sides.

"And rule number three."

Wait. Did he say three?

I swear to god if not for him finger fucking me right now, I'd tell him exactly where to take his rules, before shoving them up his ass. But, Oh. My. God. That feels good. So. Fucking. Good.

Adjusting his position, Dominique adds a third finger, working it into me, and it's almost too much.

A delicious burn spears my core as he stretches me, forcing me to accommodate all three of his fingers.

"Dom—" I'm chasing my release, sure that any minute I will spontaneously combust and I need him to give me what I need.

Instead, Dominique gives me a cruel smile, one that says he has me right where he wants me and under normal circumstances, I'd be okay with that because hell, I'm exactly where I want me to be, too. But there's an edge to his expression. A warning I'd be stupid to ignore.

"If you want to keep doing this—" He curls his fingers deep inside me, finding that spot. The one that —

...*Oh*...

I twist my hips. So close. Just a little bit more ...

He eases back, relieving some of the pressure. My shoulders slump and I release a harsh breath, a thin sheen of sweat now covering my body. "Fuck."

I was *right* there.

"You talk to someone about the shit you're dealing with." Like being dunked in a pool of ice cold water, everything in me seizes. What the hell?

Fuck that!

"No." Using my hands to shove myself up, I scoot back and scramble to get away from him. But Dominique has that look in his eyes, the one that says he is playing to win and there is no way he is going to let me get away.

Fingers slipping out of me, he wraps his hands around my calves just as I'm about to turn and dive over the edge of the bed, only instead of getting away, Dom drags me back to him, my shirt twisting beneath me as I writhe and kick, but it's no use. His grip remains tight until I'm back beneath him.

"I am not talking to some shrink," I snarl, shoving against his chest.

Dominique leans forward and braces his body over mine. I shove at him again. Not that it does even a lick of good. Dom is more than a head taller than me and at least sixty pounds of muscle heavier. He won't move unless he wants to be moved. But knowing that doesn't keep me from trying. I strike and push at his chest and I'm pretty sure I get a kick in there too. Screw the submission game. If a fight is what he's after, I'll give him one.

"I didn't say anything about a shrink," he snaps.

"Oh, so what—" I sneer, "I should talk to you, huh? Pour my heart out and let you pick up all the pieces."

His jaw flexes and I know that comment struck a chord. It's a reminder that we're not friends. Outside of the bedroom, we're not even friendly.

"I didn't say that, either." He grinds his teeth together. "Stop putting words in my mouth and listen for once in your fucking life."

"Screw you."

"I'm working on it if you'd shut the hell up and see reason."

I snap my lips together, giving him a look of pure mutiny.

There is no way I will ever willingly open up to Dominique Price. He has enough ammunition on me as it is, and I for one, am not a masochist. Showing him my most vulnerable parts is like asking to have your heart shoved through a meat grinder. No, thank you.

"So it's settled, then."

Wait. What? No, shit is not settled. I am not—

He flips me onto my stomach and pulls my hips back, leaving my ass up in the air as my shirt falls, bunching beneath my breasts.

I shove up on my hands and knees, but Dominique isn't having it. His palm presses into the center of my back, stopping me from getting very far before my face smooshes into the mattress beneath me.

"Dominique—" I growl, struggling against his hold.

He ignores me, that dominant side he likes to keep tucked away creeping out as he slides his hand over the curve of my ass and gives my backside a quick and hard slap.

I yelp, jerking forward only to be pulled back again, his hand kneading my still stinging flesh. Liquid heat pools between my thighs and it does not go unnoticed.

"You like that?" he asks right as his hand slaps me again, this time on the opposite cheek.

I curse him and squirm to get free.

"Don't argue over this," he says, both hands now massaging my ass. "You need to talk to someone."

I want to deny him, but my body betrays me, relaxing under his touch. Dominique trails his fingers lower, closer to my aching center as he massages my skin. I hold my breath, waiting for the moment when he touches me in the place I so desperately need him to. God. Why won't he just shut up and fuck me already?

"I'm not suggesting you confide in me or a shrink, but someone, Kasey. You have friends. People in your corner who want to be there for you." One hand now holds me in place—not that I'm struggling any longer—as the other toys with my clit, but Dominique makes sure to keep his touch featherlight.

"Do we have a deal?" he asks, teasing me as though his hands on my body are enough to force me to comply.

"You're not the boss of me," I grumble, but it comes out more like a groan.

Dominique increases the pressure, rubbing my clit harder and faster until my thighs shake and my stomach tightens. A needy moan escapes me. Yes. Yes. Yes.

Toes curling, the blunt end of his erection brushes along my bare skin as he climbs further onto the bed, using his knees to widen my legs while pressing forward, shoving me deeper into the mattress. My back arches as far as it'll go, my ass as high in the air as it can possibly get, and despite the awkward position, I can't help but close my eyes and give into the sensations thrumming through me.

I should feel self-conscious, bent over like this. With anyone else, I would be. But not with Dominique. I might be uncertain about his behavior outside of the bedroom. I never seem to know what he's thinking or feeling. And I sure as hell hate it when he does shit like this and tries to manipulate me to get what he wants. But when we're like this, I know without a shadow of a doubt that Dominique wants to fuck me just as badly as I want to be fucked, even if he is holding himself back in a twisted attempt to force my agreement.

Why does everything he does always feel so good? His cock brushes against me again and I press back, blindly seeking him out. I'm desperate for him to sink into me, but being the frustrating bastard that he is, he doesn't.

"I'm close," I tell him, my release barreling toward me, and as soon as the words pass my lips, I know they're the wrong ones to say.

His fingers slow, the pressure on my clit getting softer. "Dom!" I cry out.

"Those are my terms, baby girl."

I twist, trying to catch his gaze before he jerks both of my wrists behind my back and presses them with one large hand to the center of my spine. "It's a take it or leave it offer," he says, his voice laden with desire.

I squirm beneath him, rubbing my ass against whatever part of his body I can reach. His chest vibrates against my back and he grunts, jerking his own hips as far away from mine as he can get while still keeping me pressed to the bed. It's no easy feat.

"You're being unreasonable," I whine.

Proving he's not bluffing, he leans back, and I immediately miss the heat of his skin. With my wrists still in his grip, I can't move as he kneels behind me, waiting for an answer I don't want to give him.

"I'll return to class," I concede, silently cursing him.

"And?"

Grinding my molars together, I bite out, "And I'll answer your stupid phone calls."

He rewards me by shoving two fingers deep into my pussy and curling them until he finds that incredible spot that makes my breath catch.

"And?"

"And what?" I all but shout. "I agreed to what you wanted. Make me come, already."

He makes a sound of disappointment behind me and withdraws his touch from my pussy. *You have got to be fucking kidding me!*

"All or nothing." His voice is devoid of emotion.

I don't know how he does it. How he locks himself down like that. I know being hard and not finding satisfaction can't be any more pleasant than what he's putting me through right now. Urgh. He's infuriating.

"Fine." I snap. "I'll talk to someone."

Between one breath and the next, his bare cock slams into me, spearing my soaked pussy in a single, hard thrust. I cry out his name, his grip on my wrists disappearing in favor of grabbing onto my hips and using his hold for leverage as he plows into me again and again.

"Shit." I moan. "Fuck." Yes. Yes. Yes. "Right there."

Dominique fucks me like a man possessed, drilling me into the mattress. "You want to come?" he asks, a snarl in his voice.

"Yes. Please, please, please." I chant, desperate for my release.

One hand slips between my thighs to play with my clit and my orgasm rushes to the surface. Yes.

"Fuck," he curses as his hips rock into my ass and the sound of skin slapping skin echoes through the room. "So damn good."

His cock swells inside of me, signaling his impending release right as my own orgasm slams into me, pleasure rippling through every cell in my body.

I cry out his name and he slams into me three more times before lurching forward and emptying himself inside me. Chest heaving, his body shudders over mine, a low groan leaving his lips before he slips his cock free and rolls to lie next to me.

My legs give out, slipping down over the edge of the bed as I struggle to catch my breath.

Dominique looks similarly out of breath, his chest rising and falling at a rapid clip. I watch him for a moment, head turned to the side, taking in his sweat soaked skin.

I'm tempted to lean forward and lick him, but before I muster up the energy to do it, he leans up on one elbow, fists his hand in my hair, and tugs me close for a drugging kiss. It lasts only a few seconds before he releases me to sit forward.

Grabbing his discarded shirt, he uses it to wipe the sweat from his face, before getting up to head for the bathroom.

Boneless, I stay where I am, tracking his movements with my gaze when he returns seconds later with a wet washcloth in his hand. Dominique rolls me to my back and drops to his knees at the end of the bed. With the washcloth in hand, he carefully cleans the evidence of his release from between my thighs, his hooded gaze locked onto my most intimate flesh.

"So fucking pretty," he rumbles.

My cheeks heat and I look away. The look on his face is too much for me to think about right now.

With his task complete, he climbs back to his feet and tosses the rag into the corner of the room before climbing naked into bed.

"What time is it?" Eyes already closed, he tugs the blanket up to his chest and rolls to his side, getting comfortable.

I glance at the clock on his nightstand. "Almost nine," I tell him.

He grunts. "Your first class starts at 9:30. Better get moving."

I scowl at him, making no move to get up. Why does he know my schedule?

Cracking his eyes open, Dominique gives me an expectant look. He's joking. Right? The longer the seconds draw out the quicker I realize that no, Dominique is not joking.

"Today?" I demand. "You expect me to go back to school today?"

He nods and then closes his eyes. "A deal is a deal," he reminds me. "And you'd missed two weeks already. Get moving." He drives his point home by giving me a hard shove.

Un-fucking-believable.

Climbing out of bed, I take the fastest shower of my life in Dominique's bathroom before throwing on a pair of sweatpants, a tank top I had left in the guest bedroom, and stealing one of Aaron's oversized hoodies from his room.

Dominique doesn't stir even once as I scramble around his room in a rush to collect my things. He's fast asleep, his breaths even and his expression relaxed.

What an asshole.

THREE
KASEY

It turns out you only need to miss eight days of classes to start failing. Technically, I've missed more than that, but the big fat F made its appearance supposedly around day eight. My first period professor asks me to stay after class before laying into me with a lecture about prioritizing my studies and how I'm throwing my future away. And what do I do? I stand there, taking it, because what other choice do I have?

He waves his arms around, really working himself up, and it's around the ten-minute mark in his lecture when I finally snap, blurting out, "My mom just died, okay? Can you give me a fucking break?"

I press my hands over my mouth, eyes wide. Shit. I can't believe I just swore at my professor. Can he drop me from his class for that? I'm already failing, so what's he got to lose? Double shit.

I expect him to rail into me all over again with a renewed tirade, but he surprises me by leaning back in his seat, his eyes suddenly somber as he asks. "When did she pass?"

Swallowing hard, I mutter out the date of her accident, having it ingrained now in my head. How could I not? It's the day my life flipped upside down in the worst possible way.

He nods before clicking away at the mouse on his computer while I stand there, waiting for what, I'm not sure. To be excused, I suppose. Or at the very least, told if there's anything I can do? Any point in trying to finish the semester out.

Several minutes crawl by before he exhales a sigh and turns his attention from the screen back to me. "You're a running start student." He doesn't phrase it like a question, but I answer it anyway, nodding my head, not that I know why it even matters.

Being in running start means I get to finish out my senior year of high school while attending college classes and earning credits toward my—as of yet, undeclared—degree.

"What other classes are you registered for this semester?"

"English 101 and Humanities 131." Where is he going with this? Can he see my grades for my other classes too? Am I failing those ones as well?

Probably.

I haven't turned in a single assignment since Mom died, and I've shown up to maybe 2 or 3 class periods at most. I'm not sure which ones I even bothered attending. The past few weeks are mostly a blur.

My professor's brows pull together. "If you're failing my class, you're likely failing your others as well."

Pressing my lips together, I nod.

"I see here you're listed as a member of Kappa Mu."

Another nod.

"So, it won't be enough for you to simply pass," he tells me. "You need a 3.0 or better to maintain your status as a pledge."

"I'm not worried about that," I tell him. And I'm not. Sure, the Kappa Mu house is where I live right now, but it's not like I need to stay there. I'm eighteen now. I can get my own place.

With what money? The voice in my head asks.

Right. I'd need money to get my own place. Well, fuck. I only work at my aunt's diner when she needs an extra hand, and minimum wage plus tips isn't really enough to cover living expenses.

I guess I could ask Dad—I cut off that idea before it can fully form. I won't stoop to begging my dad for money, especially after he's paid my tuition and made a sizable donation to Kappa Mu to get me in. Even though I never asked him to.

"Be that as it may, you have your diploma to consider as well. If you were one of my regular students, I'd suggest you take the semester off." He offers me an apologetic smile.

"But that's not an option for you if you want to graduate on time."

Which I definitely do. Being a *super senior* is not on my bucket list.

"What options do I have?" Because from the sounds of it, it's looking pretty hopeless.

"I have your schedule. I'll speak with your other instructors and see if anything can be arranged. Your Humanities instructor won't be a problem. Ms. Blake is known for accepting make-up work when there is a justifiable reason for the delay, which you certainly have. However, Mr. Fisks..." He trails off.

"Does not accept late assignments."

His mouth twists into a grimace. "No. I'm afraid he doesn't. But give me a few days. I'm sure we can sort out an arrangement that is agreeable to all parties involved."

"Thanks," I mutter, retrieving my bag from beside my desk. It's not ideal, but it's more than I could have asked for. Mr. Fisks' class is where I'm off to next. Maybe he'll be in a good mood and I can talk to him after class and just, I don't know, beg for extra credit work.

"Miss Henderson?" My professor calls out right as I reach the door.

"Yeah?"

His brown eyes meet mine and I stiffen at the sympathy I find in his gaze. "I'm sorry for your loss. Losing one's mother is... well, there's nothing else like it. I'm sorry you're having to experience that pain at such a young age."

Pressing my lips into a grim line, I nod before rushing out of the room. Tears prick the backs of my eyes and I blink hard, desperate to banish them away, but instead of retreating, they threaten to spill over. *Dammit.*

Swiping my eyes with the backs of my hand, I keep my head down as I head for my next class, drawing up the hood on my sweater to hide my face.

Deacon is sitting in his usual spot when I arrive and I claim the seat next to him.

Eyes brightening when he sees me, he offers me a warm smile. "Hey. Long time no see. How've you been?"

That stinging sensation behind my eyes persists, so I ignore him and sink into my seat, looking everywhere else but at him. Waves of grief threaten to overwhelm me.

Why did he have to say that? Why did my professor have to pretend like he knew what I was going through? A single tear slips past my defenses to slide down my cheek and I furiously swipe it away, cursing Dominique for making me come back to class today.

I'm not ready. Doesn't he get that?

"Everything okay?" The note of concern in Deacon's voice sets me on edge.

My spine stiffens and I swallow hard. "I'm fine." I bite out the words before pulling my books from my bag, letting my hair fall forward to hide my face.

I can feel more than see Deacon as he turns to face me. "You don't seem fine," he says. "What's going on?"

Mr. Fisks comes in, saving me from having to give Deacon an answer. I'm being rude as hell, but I just — I can't. Not today. Not with him. He's so happy and smiling all the time, and I can't handle it right now. Not when I'm barely keeping my shit together.

I don't want to be here. I don't want to make small talk or have a conversation. I just want to do my work, figure out a way to pass my fucking classes so that I graduate, and go back to my room where I can pretend this is not my life right now.

"Kasey?"

I grind my teeth together.

"Kasey?" He doesn't bother to keep his voice down.

Heads turn our way and curious gazes flick between the two of us.

"Mr. Hunt?" our teacher calls out. "Do you need something?"

Deacon is still facing me, completely ignoring Mr. Fisks' thinly veiled reprimand.

"Ms. Henderson?"

I shake my head without looking up. "No. Sorry." I mumble.

"Alright then. Today we'll be covering—" I don't hear the rest of what he says because the next thing I know, Deacon's pulling me to my feet, throwing me over his shoulder, and stalking out of the room.

"Mr. Hunt!" Fisks exclaims.

Our classmates snicker. A few whistle and make catcalling sounds. And me, I hang like a limp noodle on Deacon's shoulder, not even bothering to put up a fight because what would be the point?

The halls are nearly empty when we exit the classroom. Deacon makes his way down a more secluded hallway before setting me on my feet and as soon as my feet touch the ground, I move to leave but Deacon turns me to face him, hands gripping my shoulders so I can't get away.

"What's going on with you today?" His voice is soft, soothing, and something about the concern in his voice makes a fresh wave of tears spring into my eyes.

Dammit.

Deacon shoves my hood back and wipes my messy hair away from my face, tucking it behind my ears so he can get a better look at me.

Averting my gaze, I blink hard, desperate to keep my emotions at bay. It's only my first day back.

"Hey."

I jerk away from him.

"Hey." He tries again, leading me over to a bench with a hand on the small of my back. "Talk to me. Does this have anything to do with Price?"

I bark out a humorless laugh and shake my head. Boy problems are the least of my worries right now.

"Okay. Okay." He's quiet for a moment before asking, "This the same stuff you were dealing with before when I found you during practice?"

Swallowing hard, I consider denying it, but again, what would be the point? So instead, I give him a single nod. A few days after Mom died, Dominique had to go in for practice, which normally wouldn't matter, except he was in full-on hovering mode—understandably. I was a wreck at the time. He dragged me to practice with him, refusing to leave me at home alone and I was too out of it to bother fighting him on it.

He'd stashed me in one of the media rooms the team uses for watching game footage when I got a call from Aaron and the next thing I knew, I was a blubbering mess, hyperventilating and having what I can only assume was a panic attack. My ears were ringing and I could hardly breathe.

But then Deacon showed up and threw a bunch of chocolate at me to make me feel better. It was weird. He has no real reason to look out for me. But it was also sweet. And in the moment, it was what I needed.

Deacon didn't ask questions. He didn't pry. He was just... there. No expectations. No demands. He kept me company until Dominique came to collect me and did what he could to help.

"Do you want to talk about it?" he asks.

Narrowing my eyes, I glower at him. "Fuck no."

Deacon exhales a harsh breath of relief. "Thank fuck." He runs a hand over his face. "I was worried there for a second."

"You were worried?" I raise a brow and sniff, some of the weight lifting from my chest.

He smirks. "Obviously. I mean, I'm here if you need to talk, but I'm gonna be real with you. I suck at the emotional shit. Especially with girls. When chicks get sad and then cry," he shivers dramatically, "Do you have any idea how uncomfortable that is for a dude?"

I snort. "Way to be all empathetic and shit."

"No really. What are we supposed to do?" he asks. "We can't fix it, right? Whatever it is that—"

"My mom died," I blurt out for the second time today.

"Fuck."

"Yup."

Deacon doesn't miss a beat. "See what I mean? What is a guy supposed to do with that?"

"Nothing I guess." I shrug.

"And that is why talking about feelings fucking sucks. Nothing gets fixed."

A smile curls the corners of my mouth. "I've been saying the same thing to my friends, but they won't drop it and leave me alone. Everyone wants me to talk about what I'm going through." I worry my bottom lip. Why won't they accept I don't need to talk about it? I just need to figure out a way to move on.

Deacon's expression screws into a look of horror. "That right there is some bullshit," he tells me. "Your mom died. You handle that however you need to, and if *not* talking about it is the way to go, then that's the path you take. No one else gets to decide how you need to cope with your shit." He shakes his head. "Idiots. All of them."

I laugh. It's small and unexpected, but also makes the tight feeling in my chest loosen a little bit more.

"Thank you," I tell him, meaning it.

"Anytime. I'm here for you." He winks. "But we'll leave the emotional chit chat to the pros. Or—" his smile widens, "we come up with fun shit to do to distract you and maybe stir up a little trouble along the way."

My brows lift. "What did you have in mind?" Because I am one hundred percent on board for distractions.

"You'll see. But first, let's go find you some chocolate."

"What is this called again?" I ask, eyeing the black box with the white ball mounted in the middle of it. He's plugged it into a projector that we've propped up with a stack of our books and is currently looking for a power source to plug it into.

"Golden Tee," Deacon says, scanning the wall at our backs before meeting my gaze. "Pretty epic, right?"

I humor him with a smile, what feels like my first genuine one in ages, before rolling my eyes at him with a small laugh. "Yep. The best thing since sliced bread," I say, giving his setup a curious side eye. I've never heard of this game before, but he's been bouncing like a kid in a candy store ever since I agreed to play. He mentioned something about it being a bar game, but since we're both underage and can't very well walk into one of the local bars to play, I guess having a version of your own is the next best thing.

After leaving Fisks' class, I blindly agreed to play this game on the promise that it was fun and that Deacon would swipe a six-pack for us to share while we played because while he might be underage, most of his fraternity is not.

With booze on the table, saying yes was a no-brainer. We swung by the Alpha Ze frat house to grab this weird gaming console, a portable projector, and a white sheet along with the six-pack of Blue Moon, and away we went. Not going to lie, I'm not a fan of beer. Blue Moon is better than the kind my brother drinks. There's a slight orange flavor to it. But it's still beer. Not that that stops me from drinking it. I'm here for distractions, after all.

Once we had all the necessities, we went back to my place. We could have stayed at his frat house, but a lot of the guys he lives with take evening and online classes, so it was busier than the Kappa Mu house is during the day. And while I want to take my mind off things, I don't particularly feel like socializing with a bunch of strangers and pretending everything is just a bucket of sunshine and rainbows right now.

"Yes!" Deacon exclaims, having found one of the exterior outlets along the side of the house. After dumping our bags in my room, we decided to set up shop on the side patio where we'd have a bit more privacy than we would if we were in the main part of the backyard. I'm pretty sure only Quinn and Isla are around, and would probably leave us alone if I asked them to, but I don't know how long we'll be here or when the rest of the girls get out of their classes, so this is the safer bet.

"Okay. That should do it," he tells me, taking the gaming box from my hands and hitting the power button on both it and the projector.

"So this is virtual..." I trail off, still not seeing how a black box with a ball somehow translates into—

"Golf. Trust me, it's fun." He offers me a toothy grin. "Way better than real golf."

This isn't what I had in mind when I said I was down for a distraction, but I'm going to take his word for it. And he did deliver on the chocolate at least. Though for the record, it makes beer taste even more like shit. Never would have guessed it was possible

With the sheet pinned up on the back fence, a virtual field spreads out before us across its surface.

"So, here's what you do."

Deacon gives me a quick rundown of how the console works, how points are awarded, and offers a few tips for getting your ball around curves while dealing with virtual wind. It sounds easy enough, only my first few attempts are complete and utter failures. I keep swinging my ball into the sandpits or the lake, and it doesn't take long before Deacon is absolutely smoking me.

But three beers in and twenty minutes later, I finally start to get the hang of it.

"There you go!" Deacon cheers, giving me a high five when I land my ball in the hole on the third swing. "That's what I'm talking about!"

I grin, accepting his praise before handing over the console for him to take his next turn. There is zero chance of me beating—let alone catching up to—his score, but despite my competitive nature, I realize I don't care about winning. I can't remember the last time I had this much fun losing at something.

Deacon misses his mark and drives his ball into a pile of bushes on the screen. The booze seems to have improved my game, but it's made his worse.

I'll remember that for next time.

He's a good sport about the miss, throwing his head back with a laugh as his character fights through the virtual shrubbery to retrieve his ball.

With his head thrown back, my eyes are drawn to the designs that decorate his neck. He has a cross tattooed on the left side. A scroll design filled with script on his right. Most of his skin, or at least what I've seen of it, is heavily inked, both forearms decorated with designs. Having seen him during practice, I know both calves are covered in tattoos as well.

"When did you start getting ink?" I ask, tipping my head toward him. Deacon is only a year, maybe two, older than I am, and he has a lot of tats already for somebody so young. I'm no tattoo expert, but some of his pieces I know took multiple sessions, and I can't imagine he'd have this much ink completed if he bothered to wait until he was eighteen to start.

"Dunno. Sometime in high school, I guess." He gives me a curious look, his honey-colored eyes meeting mine before his mouth quirks into a mischievous grin that is both devastating and unnerving. "Why? Do you like what you see?" he asks, taking a step closer.

I roll my eyes, giving his chest a light shove when he takes another step, invading my personal space. "Like I'd tell you if I did," I quip.

I'm not interested in Deacon Hunt. Not in that way. But only an idiot can't see how attractive he is. Deacon is a Kelly Oubre Jr doppelgänger if ever there is one. Medium brown skin, light golden eyes, and thick black hair. He's mixed. Half black or better.

He has full lips, a sharp jaw, and a leaner build than Dominique, but he's just as physically fit. And the look he's giving me is one I'd bet gets him whatever he wants. It's a panty dropping smolder. One I'm pleasantly surprised I'm immune to.

"Oh, yeah?" Deacon raises one brow, his expression growing more interested. "Why is that?" He drops his voice a few octaves and intensifies his smoldering look. At least, I think his aim is a smolder. I'm not entirely sure. Deacon is a flirt, and I'm pretty sure he doesn't come with an off switch. But most of the time, his flirting is directed elsewhere. He flirted with me at the start, when we first met, but I made it clear I was only interested in friendship and he seemed on board with that.

Shortly after, Dominique made it a point to inform Deacon, physically and aggressively, that I was off limits. Something I didn't appreciate. Especially given we weren't even hooking up at the time, so Dominique had zero justification for being an overprotective dick like that. But he, Roman, and Emilio, Aaron's other two best friends and my surrogate brothers, opted to join in on Dominique's crusade to scare Deacon away from me and went out of their way to drive their point home every day on the field during practice until Deacon got with the program.

I can't say I blame him. I might reconsider who I spent my time with too if it was me getting my ass handed to me on the football field everyday just for being friendly. But that doesn't mean I was happy about it.

It was frustrating, to say the least. I don't have many friends here and Deacon went from wanting to hangout to ignoring my existence, all to avoid Dominique and the other guys' wrath without ever filling me in on what the hell was behind his cold shoulder.

He ghosted me and it sucked.

But eventually, he came around, realizing that what the guys were pulling was bullshit. Which it was. He showed up at a Kappa Mu party and told me about the whole mess, letting the chips fall where they may. Suffice it to say, I was pissed and what happened next wasn't pretty.

Dominique and I had a heated exchange. I take issue with people dictating my life and making decisions about what's best for me, so I put a stop to Dom's interference.

Tension between Dominique and Deacon is still high. Neither one of them are fans of the other. I doubt they'll ever come close to becoming friends, but there's an unsteady truce between them, at least. One that I'm pretty sure survives with the understanding that Dominique won't make Deacon's life a living hell so long as Deacon sticks to being friends with me and nothing more.

Which begs the question, what the hell is he doing right now?

"Are you drunk?" I ask.

We blew through the six-pack before grabbing a bottle of Malibu Rum from the Kappa Mu kitchen—a much better choice if you ask me—and while I have a pleasant buzz, I figured it'd take more before Deacon lost his head.

"Nope," he tells me.

"Riiiight." I take a step back. But just the one. "Then what are you doing?"

His expression shifts and he turns back to the game, sliding his hand back across the ball on the console before slamming it forward in a hard swipe that sends his virtual golf ball sailing through the air. "Winning," he says with a grin, the heated look on his face disappearing to be replaced with a carefree smile.

I open my mouth to call bullshit when the back door leading inside pops open and Quinn pokes her head outside.

"Hey, you!" she calls and I turn, giving her my attention. "Some of the girls and I are going to go dress shopping for the McIntire dinner. Wanna come?"

I have no clue what that even is.

"I'm good," I say before adding a "Thanks, though," to soften the rejection, because even though I doubt she really wants me there, Quinn is a softy, and I'd hate to inadvertently hurt her feelings.

She's my *Big* here at Kappa Mu—the sorority sister and upperclassman tasked with helping me to fit in—so while I appreciate the invite, she's only asking out of obligation. Not because she and I are close or anything. We could be, I think. We get along well, and I've spent enough time with her to know the foundation for friendship is there. But with everything going on in my life, I don't have it in me to invest that kind of time or mental energy into a new friendship. I barely have it in me to drag myself out of bed. Something she and my other housemates have obviously noticed, but have gratefully not bothered to ask me about.

Besides, I'm not the kind of girl who enjoys shopping for the hell of it. I'd only bring the group vibe down.

"Okay. If you change your mind, give me a call and I'll let you know where we're at."

I nod, promising I will, even though I know I won't.

Her attention shifts to Deacon.

"Are you taking—" she begins, but Deacon surprises me by cutting her off.

"Nah. She's spoken for." He lifts one shoulder in a shrug.

Quinn's brows pull together into a frown.

Who are they talking about?

"So who are you taking, then?" To what? Is this some weird fraternity slash sorority thing I'm not privy to as a freshman or something?

"No worries. I'm covered," he tells her.

My eyes ping-pong back and forth between them. I feel like I'm missing something. I didn't even realize they knew each other. Though I guess it shouldn't surprise me. At the last pool party our house threw, I all but shoved her in his direction after she made her interest clear, suggesting she shoot her shot. I never really saw what came of that, since shortly after Dominique and my brother—Aaron—showed up. But I mean, there could be something going on there, though I'm not getting *relationship* or even *we slept together* vibes from these two. More like... friendly acquaintances, maybe?

Quinn's shoulders drop, her expression now one of disappointment. "Oh. Okay. Well, if things fall through, let me know. I have a friend—"

"I will," he assures her.

She tells me goodbye and closes the door, presumably to head out and go shopping. That was... weird. I consider asking Deacon what all that was about, but as I think about it, I realize I don't care.

I'd rather just get back to the game, so that's what we do, previous conversation and awkwardness set aside and forgotten.

FIVE
DOMINIQUE

I t's just after four in the afternoon when I make it back to my place after my classes, my last one having run later than usual. Aaron is home when I arrive, sitting on the sofa with his hands folded beneath his chin, expression blank. According to the flight plan, his plane landed around one this afternoon.

I wanted to be here when he got back, but I had a quiz in two of my classes, so skipping today wasn't an option. I reasoned with myself that Aaron wouldn't be alone for long. Between waiting for baggage claim and dealing with traffic, he'd be home for two and a half hours at most before I got here, but seeing him now, I get the sinking feeling I made a big fucking mistake.

I should have been here. Hell, I should have insisted on picking him up from the airport instead of letting him catch a ride share home. I know how he gets sometimes, and I should have seen this coming.

At the very least, I could have called one of our friends to meet him here. I could have made sure he wasn't alone. He'd have been pissed. No full-grown man appreciates being assigned a babysitter, but he would have gotten over it. Eventually.

"Hey, man," I call out, dropping my bag by the door. I step further into the room, waiting for him to acknowledge my presence.

He doesn't.

Aaron's eyes are trained on a small urn that sits in the center of our coffee table in front of him. Mouth pressed into a flat line, his gaze is so focused it's almost like he's afraid the thing will walk off on its own if he so much as looks away.

The urn containing his mother's remains is maybe eight inches tall and three inches wide. I don't know why, but I expected it to be bigger.. Knowing a grown woman is ash inside of that thing is unsettling. Would I fit in something like that? Is that really all that's left when we die?

"Everything okay?" It's like Aaron doesn't even hear me. His attention never moves from his mother's remains.

Knowing he can sometimes zone out like this, I walk across the room, making it a point to stomp, so he hears my steps as I pass in front of him, only his gaze never shifts in my direction.

Well, fuck.

I don't want to spook him. If he's lost in his head right now, any loud noises or sudden movements can set him off. Aaron struggles with PTSD, and given what he's been through, I shouldn't be surprised to find him like this. Which makes me even more pissed with myself because, like I said, I should have expected it. Should have made better fucking arrangements. My friend needed me and I wasn't here for him.

I don't have a lot of options here since I can't very well leave him like this. I tried that once during freshman year after we started living together. Things were still rocky between us, so I didn't know all the shit he was dealing with back then, but I remember coming home after practice one day to find him on the porch.

It was maybe three or four in the afternoon. I said hi, and when he didn't respond, I let him be. I was too tired from training to dwell on his behavior and figured he was pissed off at me over something stupid and would talk to me eventually.

I went about the rest of my day, thinking he'd come in at some point. And when he didn't I assumed he left. Went to the skate park or something.

At no point did I think he could still be out there, sitting on the porch like some frozen statue.

It wasn't until close to midnight when I opened the front door to check and see if his car was still in the driveway, thinking he might have left without me realizing it, that I saw he'd never moved from his original spot.

He'd sat there for close to nine hours without ever realizing how much time was passing by.

I didn't know better back then. Had no fucking idea about the kind of shit going on in his head. All I remember is reaching down to shake his shoulder and the next thing I know, my head snaps back and I'm seeing stars.

Aaron threw one hell of a right hook at my face, catching me square in the jaw, and never in my life have I taken a hit quite like that. It took several seconds for my hearing and vision to come back, leaving me more vulnerable than I've ever been.

Thankfully, his swift reaction to my touch snapped him out of whatever funk he was in. There've been times when it didn't—not with me but with other people—when Aaron kept on punching, not seeing who it was in front of him, until someone physically pulled him off of a body.

He told me once that he rarely remembers what he's thinking about or why he feels the need to lash out. He just does.

For him, it's almost like he's asleep one minute and drowning in adrenaline the next. His fight-or-flight instinct rears its head, and no matter what, for Aaron, he's always going to fight. It's a subconscious decision he has no control over.

I have fast as fuck reflexes thanks to playing football, but that night, I swear, I never saw him move. It took six months after that before he told me what the hell was wrong with him, so now, I can't say I know what I should do, but I know what not to do.

Dropping to the ground, I crouch on the opposite side of the coffee table, his mother's urn between us. When his eyes refuse to flick in my direction, I reach out, my movements slow, and wrap my hand around the cool metal, sliding the urn back a few inches before letting it go.

His left eye twitches, but it's the only reaction I get, so I do it again. Only this time, I move it to the right, forcing him to turn his gaze if he wants to keep it in his line of sight.

Instead of moving, he blinks several times. Some of the fog lifts from his gaze. It's weird, like watching someone come back into their body.

"You good?" I ask, careful to keep my voice pitched low.

His lashes flutter, his blinks coming quicker now, and I see the exact moment when he comes back to himself. His jaw goes rigid, nostrils flaring.

He's always pissed off at first. The adrenaline dump hits him no matter what, only like this, he doesn't have a target to strike out at. Aaron has enough sense of self to hold himself in check, long enough to realize he's not in any danger. There is no threat. But that doesn't mean any of this is easy for him.

Seconds pass between us in silence before he exhales a loud breath.

His eyes meet mine before flitting away in shame. Grinding my teeth together, I keep my mouth shut. There aren't any words I can offer that will make him feel better, and in the past, acknowledging the turmoil raging inside him only made matters worse.

"How long?" His voice cracks and he swallows hard, refusing to meet my gaze.

"Not long," I say, hoping he'll leave it at that.

His nostrils flare again, color warming his cheeks. "How long?" he demands.

I kick myself for not having a better answer. For not being here to make sure this shit didn't happen. He's been doing good. And I don't know how he'll handle a setback like this.

"An hour. Maybe two." I consider lying but think better of it. Aaron lets me in when shit goes sideways, because we have that level of trust with one another. I won't risk that just to soften one blow.

He nods, expression grim. "What time is it?"

"Just after four."

Working his jaw, he shoves to his feet and I follow suit. It's like Aaron to bolt when he has an episode and that is the one thing I do not want him to do right now. He clenches and unclenches his fists at his sides, expression hard.

Self-loathing and frustration flicker across his face.

"I was going to grab something to eat." Really, I planned to hit the shower before tracking down Kasey, but no way am I leaving Aaron to wallow in self-pity like this. Nor can I risk him going off the rails because he had an episode. "Give me five minutes to change out of my practice clothes and we can swing by the Sun Valley station."

He doesn't respond, not that I expected him to. But he doesn't move to leave either. Good. He's processing shit, and with any luck, he'll be here when I get out of the shower.

I'm inclined to hover. Make sure he's okay. But Aaron doesn't need that from me. He needs to know shit like this happens. That I won't judge him for it. And that he's going to be okay. This is a minor setback. Nothing more.

Ten minutes later, I'm freshly showered and changed and Aaron stands in the same spot I left him, though he doesn't have that hollow and angry look on his face anymore.

Progress.

"All set?" I ask, grabbing my keys from the counter.

"Yeah," he tells me, following me outside to my Escalade. "But I need to make a detour."

"Cool. Where to?" He could ask me to drive him to timbuktu and I'd do it.

Turning on the ignition, I'm backing out of our shared driveway when he says, "Swing by Kasey's. I've been a shit brother. I need to check in on my sister."

Flexing my hands on the steering wheel, I head for her place. I'd like to check in on her too, only without an audience. Whatever. It is what it is. It's not like Aaron will know I'm banging her just by looking at her, right?

He keeps his eyes trained out the window as we eat up the few blocks between our place and the Kappa Mu sorority house. Kasey's room is near the side exit, so instead of parking out front, I swing around the back only to find an unfamiliar car parked in the usually empty space beside her Subaru WRX.

"What the hell?"

"What's wrong?"

Shit. I didn't mean to say that out loud. Killing the engine, I shake my head and get out of my SUV. "Nothing. Sorry, man. Just didn't recognize the car."

Aaron gets out, closing the door behind him as we both size up the ride. It's a two-door Chevy Silverado.

"Could belong to one of the other girls," Aaron says.

My lip curls. Unlikely. The truck is black on black. A glossy body finish with matte black wheels and a blackout grill. It's an older body style. I'd put it somewhere around 2010-2015 if I had to guess, but whoever owns it took the time to do a few custom upgrades. Few chicks are going to pay that kind of attention to their ride.

"That shit belongs to a dude." And given that only Kasey parks on this side of the house, the guy in question came to see her. Who?

"I wasn't gone long." True. He wasn't. A little less than a week. "Is she dating someone now?" Aaron doesn't seem bothered by the idea.

Working my jaw, I glare at him before shaking my head. "Not that I'm aware of." It takes everything in me to keep my voice flat. Emotionless. It won't do any good letting on to the fact that the very idea of Kasey dating anyone pisses me right the hell off.

We're not in a relationship, but we agreed. This shit is exclusive, and I expect her to stick to that.

Aaron shrugs. "Maybe it's new. I mean," —he smirks, some of the light coming back in his eyes— "not like she'd tell you, anyway. Right, man? You two hate each other."

Sucking on my teeth, I'm saved from having to respond when a feminine laugh draws mine and Aaron's attention away from the truck.

"She sounds good," he says before turning.

We cut across the lot, following the sound of the voice. I know without needing to see her that it belongs to Kasey, even without Aaron's confirmation. And he's right. She does sound good.

A smile curls the corners of my mouth, knowing she's enjoying herself. It was a good idea to push her today. For a second there, I worried that returning to school would be too hard for her, but from the sounds of it—

We turn the corner and I come to a hard stop. *The fuck?*

Ice trickles through my veins at the sight of the guy standing next to her. Way too fucking close for comfort.

"Who is that?" Aaron asks, taking in the scene in front of us.

My spine stiffens, my blood all of a sudden heating like an inferno. "A fucking dead man," I grind out, and the next thing

I know, my feet are moving and I'm eating up the distance between us as I stalk toward Deacon and Kasey.

Her back is to me so she doesn't see our approach, but Deacon must feel my gaze burning holes into his back because he looks over his shoulder, and as soon as our eyes meet, he blanches.

Good. That asshole should be scared. I warned him to stay away from her. Just because the team is no longer pummeling his ass during practice doesn't mean he has the all clear from me and can just move in and make a pass at Kasey. She's still off-fucking-limits.

He leans over, whispering something in her ear and getting way too fucking close to her. Rage clouds my vision. If he doesn't back away from her right now, I'm going to make him regret ever transferring to Suncrest U. He must see the threat in my gaze because he takes a step back right as Kasey's head snaps in my direction.

A look of surprise colors her expression before her blue eyes narrow. And what does she do? Arms folded over her chest, she takes a step forward, in front of Deacon. I almost laugh. The pretty little idiot. If this is her bullshit attempt at protecting him, she's going to need more than her five-foot-three frame to stop me.

I'll be damned if I let Deacon, or anyone else for that matter, try to take what's *mine*.

SIX

D eacon leans close to whisper in my ear. "We've got company." Inclining his head, toward our cars, I follow his gaze to find Dominique stalking toward me. Eyes hard and footsteps determined. He looks like a man on a warpath. Muscles flex with each step he takes and his face is stony, hard lines carved into his handsome face but it's his eyes that unsettle me.

They burn with an intensity that screams there is hell to pay. I get the feeling I'm the one who will be on the receiving end of it.

My smile slips from my face. *This should be fun.* Shifting my weight, I place myself between him and Deacon before he gets the chance to do anything stupid. But another look at his face says that was the wrong move. *Shit.* His already murderous expression darkens.

A few steps behind him is my brother, Aaron, moving at a more relaxed pace. Our eyes meet, his green ones softening at the sight of me. Something inside my chest lightens. *He's here!* Without thinking, I sprint toward him, blowing past a pissed-off Dominique, who stops in his tracks to watch as I jump into my brother's outstretched arms, wrapping my legs around his waist as I hug him for all I'm worth.

"Hey, baby sis." Aaron buries his face in my hair, squeezing me tight. "I missed you."

"I missed you, too." Until this moment, I didn't realize how much.

Having him back makes the tight ache in my chest loosen enough that it no longer hurts to breathe. Burying my nose in his neck, I suck in a lungful of air, taking comfort in the pear and cedar wood scent that is my brother. I never thought I'd love the smell of his Axe body spray so much.

"You been staying out of trouble?" Aaron places me back on my feet before ruffling my curly blond hair.

Swatting his hand away, I scowl at him before pushing my hair out of my face. "I never get in trouble," I retort. Lies. I've gotten in *some* trouble. But nothing Aaron needs to worry about.

He chuckles, and that tight feeling in my chest loosens a little more. It's good to see him smiling. I'm sure he's had a hell of a week, but he looks good. Better than I could have hoped for.

"Is that why Dom looked ready to commit murder as soon as he spotted your friend over there?" He tips his head behind me, giving me a curious look, and I remember Deacon is still here.

Aaron quirks a brown, obviously waiting for an introduction so I give him one, laughing his comment aside with a roll of my eyes.

"He's the second string quarterback." I tell him, thinking on my feet. "He's giving Dom a run for his money so they don't really get along but," I shrug, "Not many people get along with Dominique, so what can you expect?"

My brother takes the bait. Thank god. I don't know what the hell Dominique was thinking but he's coming off as a jealous boyfriend and that shit is not going to fly. Is he trying to out what's going on between us?

Bending at the waist, Aaron laughs, his shaggy blond hair falling over the front of his face. When he catches his breath, he runs his fingers through it, pushing the strands back from his eyes before closing the distance between him and his friend.

I fall into step beside him, careful to keep a wary gaze on Dominique. He hasn't said anything—yet. And I'm praying he keeps his mouth shut and doesn't give us away. The look on his face is bad enough. Who knows the damage he can cause if he opens that stupid mouth of his.

"She's got you there," Aaron says to Dominique. "You can be prickly."

Dominique glowers, but doesn't answer, his attention still locked on Deacon, who seems to have adopted the *if I don't move, no one will notice me* approach. I sigh. It's a little late for that.

"Relax, man," Aaron says before turning to me and asking, "So, does your friend have a name?"

"Yeah. This is—"

"Deacon." He steps up beside me and holds his hand out to my brother. "Deacon Hunt."

Aaron shakes it, eyes sharpening. There is the overprotective brother I know and love.

"Nice. I'm Aaron. Kasey's very protective older brother." At least he doesn't bother to deny it.

"I feel you there, man. I've got three little sisters of my own." He chuckles. "I know how that goes."

Aaron's shoulders relax a fraction as he withdraws his hand, still giving Deacon a considering look. "Three. I've got my hands full with this one." His smile widens. "How do you two know each other?" To me, he adds, "I thought you avoided fraternizing with ball players?"

Isn't he funny? "Only the ones who make it a point to tell me what to do." I give Dominique a pointed look. "And we met in class. Deacon's helping me study while I play catch up for the days I've missed."

"That better be all he's helping you with," Dominique grumbles, low enough that Aaron doesn't hear.

"So you two are..." Aaron trails off, leaving Deacon or I to fill in the blank.

Only neither of us do. As the silence stretches between us, the tension in the air grows thick and uncomfortable. Dominique looks two seconds away from exploding. I need to say something.

"We're friends," Deacon finally answers. "Just friends." The second statement he delivers with his eyes locked on Dominique, as though some silent communication passes between them.

Dominique nods, like whatever message Deacon was trying to relay was received. *So stupid.*

Rolling my eyes, I ignore them both. Men are such idiots sometimes.

Shoving his hands into his pockets, Aaron rocks back on his heels, digesting Deacon's words before offering a noncommittal, "Cool," and taking in the Golden-Tee set up behind us. "Doesn't look like much studying is going on." He nods toward the image behind us, projected on the sheet.

"Brain break," I tell him. "Deacon is teaching me to play virtual gold. It's actually sorta fun."

"Golden Tee?" my brother asks, his green eyes brightening.

"Yeah, you play?" Deacon asks.

"Bro, I'm a beast. I hold the top score at the Stadium." The Stadium is a campus bar where everyone likes to hangout when there isn't a party or game to attend. I haven't been but I hear the girls talk about it enough to know it's one of the more popular hangouts.

"No shit. You're Sk8ro3?"

A broad smile splits my brother's face. "That's me." And just like that, the two of them start talking about the game becoming fast friends. Deacon passes him a controller and Aaron takes over my spot as player two.

With their backs turned and their attention focused on the game, I feel more than see Dominique move up behind me, a malevolent presence intent on stealing the oxygen from my lungs.

"What game are you playing at, baby girl?" His voice is deceptively calm, but I don't miss the thread of warning in his tone. He's pissed. Not that I'm surprised. I know Deacon is on his list of least favorite people. But it's not like I expected him to drop by unannounced. I didn't plan for this.

I try not to focus on how close he is—close enough for me to smell his cologne. Cinnamon and sandalwood. And instead, pay attention to breathing, desperate to slow my racing heart.

"I'm not playing any game," I snap, keeping my voice low so it doesn't reach my brother.

Gripping my hips, Dominique jerks me back until I'm pressed to his front.

"Why is he here?" He leans forward, nose trailing over my exposed skin.

I shiver and go to step away, but his grip tightens, holding me in place.

"What are you doing?" I hiss, eyes watching my brother. He can look in this direction at any time. All it would take is a second, and we'd be caught.

"Answer the question." One hand slips under the hem of my shirt to rest against my lower belly. His hold is possessive, his touch like a hot brand against my skin.

"You told me to talk to someone," I remind him.

His fingers dig into the flesh of my abdomen for a millisecond before he relaxes them. "And you chose *him*?"

He's seething, and I can't help the smile that ghosts over my lips. It's a good thing he can't see the expression on my face.

"Yup."

"Careful," he warns. "You're walking a dangerous line. One that's liable to get you punished."

A tiny bead of sweat forms along my hairline. It's not overly warm outside. Yet, I'm burning up.

"You can't punish me for doing what you asked." *Right?* Though a part of me isn't as turned off by the idea as I should be. Anticipation thrums through my veins.

"Watch me," he growls low in my ear before sliding his hand over my flat tummy and into the front of my jeans.

Clenching my thighs together, I ignore the heat blossoming in my chest. The memory of my morning with Dominique floods through my mind and despite my efforts to keep my body rigid against his, he makes no sign of being deterred. If anything, my lack of response only serves to embolden him.

Dominique slides a finger over the fabric of my already damp panties before rubbing my clit through the material. Shit. I clench my teeth, fighting against the urge to whimper.

His teeth nip at my earlobe as he strokes me, sending a bright burst of pleasure straight to my center. The air hums with electricity and his lean and powerful form wraps around mine.

"I'll be back tonight after Aaron goes to bed." His tone is laced with promise. "Leave the side door unlocked."

I swallow hard, keeping utterly still despite the demands of my body, urging me to give in to his touch. To welcome his embrace.

"Wear nothing but my shirt when I arrive. I want you ready for me. Understand?"

My hands curl into fists at my sides. I can't breathe. Let alone form coherent words to respond. Deacon and my brother are only a few yards away. At any point, one or both of them can turn around to find Dominique's hand buried down the front of my pants, and for some strange, fucked up reason, knowing that only turns me on more.

My lungs expand with my attempts to suck in a breath.

"Tell me you understand, baby girl."

He flicks my clit, eliciting a whimper that is met by his dark chuckle. "Good enough," he says and withdraws his hand from my panties.

A choked sound of disappointment escapes me, and it's then that my brother turns to glance in our direction. "You two good?" he asks, attention split between us and the game.

"All good, man," Dominique answers, standing stiff behind me.

How does he sound so unaffected right now? Turning so my flushed face doesn't give me away, I call out, "I'm gonna hit the books while you guys play, but call me later. K'?"

I don't know if my words are meant for Deacon or my brother, but both promise to talk to me later, waving me off as they shout at the display, redirecting their focus back to the game.

Dominique's heated gaze spears arrows of awareness into my back as I head for the door but I refuse to look over my shoulder.

Don't look at him. I tell myself. *It'll only give him what he wants.*

Chewing my bottom lip, I open the exterior door that leads inside. I've barely passed the threshold when the urge to look back damn near overwhelms me. *You can do this, Kasey. Just close the door.*

I need to turn around to close the door. So I do, careful to keep my gaze downcast. But I also need to make sure it closes all the way. Quinn would be annoyed with me if I left it cracked and let all of the cool air out.

It's the excuse I tell myself but I know it's a lie. Just like it's a lie when I tell myself that not only am I strong enough to keep from meeting his gaze, no part of me wants to meet it anyway.

Lie. Lie. Lie.

And like a glutton for the punishment he's warned of, I give in to the impulse to lift my head as I push against the door.

Our gazes zero in on one another and his dark stare flickers, tracking my every move.

For a long second, I'm trapped under the weight of his gaze. An invisible hold taking over me.

His mouth curls into a cruel smile. It promises pleasure, sparking an involuntary shiver. But maybe ... maybe it also promises a little pain.

True to my word, I hit my books and play catch up on some of my classwork, but time moves agonizingly slow as I wait for Dominique to arrive. Pinpricks of nervous energy buzz beneath my skin. I can't get thoughts of him out of my mind, which is both a good and a bad thing.

Good, because it means I'm not dwelling on the clusterfuck that is my life right now. But bad because Dominique Price should never take up this much of my head space. *Ever.*

Teeth clenching in irritation, I redirect my attention to the work spread before me, scribbling in my notebook as I reread a passage in my textbook for what feels like the hundredth time.

But no matter how hard I try to focus on my work, my thoughts continue straying back to Dominique. Urgh. Why? He's not that interesting.

Dominique Price is arrogant. Domineering. He insists on telling me what to do. Who I can and can't hangout with. He has the misguided notion that he has any say in how I live my life. And here I am, putting up with it.

"It's just sex," I say out loud.

Great, amazing, mind-blowing sex. But at the end of the day, it is still only sex.

"Don't read into it."

The fact that seeing me with Deacon pisses Dominique off says nothing to how he feels about me. He's not jealous. Dominique doesn't get jealous.

We've played this song and dance before. He's possessive, but that has more to do with his animosity toward Deacon than it does with any interest in me.

This is no strings attached sex. Nothing less. Nothing more. Exactly how I want it to be.

Knock. Knock.

The pounding at my door startles me from my thoughts and I curse, realizing I haven't changed since coming inside. What will he do when he sees I ignored his demand to be dressed in nothing but one of his shirts, waiting?

And why does the thought of pissing him off make my core clench in eager anticipation?

He warned he would punish me.

What does he have in mind? Will the punishment be worse for this slight?

Do I care?

Climbing from my bed where I have my school books scattered, I walk over to my bedroom door, eyeing it with wary expectation. I could ignore him. Pretend I'm not here.

Considering it, my eyes stray to the clock on my nightstand. That can't be right. Brows furrowed, I realize it's only a little after six.

Aaron wouldn't be in bed this early. At least, I don't think he would.

There's a chance he called it an early night, what with traveling and jet lag, but seeing him earlier, I didn't get the feeling he was running on fumes.

And if Aaron is still up, that means it's not Dominique at my door. Who—

The doorknob twists to swing open on silent hinges.

"Knock, knock," Deacon calls out, pushing my bedroom door wide before stepping into the room.

I freeze, momentarily thrown by his unexpected appearance.

"Hey." Snapping out of my stupor, I offer him a small wave. "I thought you'd left."

Deacon shakes his head and closes the door behind him before leaning against it. "That eager to be rid of me?" he asks with a quirk of his brow.

Rolling my eyes, I go back to my bed and begin putting away my books, tucking my scribbled notes between the pages so I don't lose my place.

"No, but I abandoned you with Dominique and my brother," I remind him. "If you were smart, you'd have found an excuse to bail. Did they only just leave?"

Damn. That means he was stuck hanging out with them for over an hour. A shiver of guilt trickles down my spine. *Way to look out, Kasey. Just throw Deacon to the wolves, why don't you?*

Is he pissed with me now? Is that why he stopped by my room?

"Nah. Dom hung around for maybe five minutes after you left. But Aaron stuck it out. Your brother's a cool dude. We played a few rounds before he had to bounce to meet up with some friends for food. He invited me to tag along, but I figured Dom would be there and—" he shrugs, "—you know how he is."

Okay. Phew. At least he wasn't with Dominique this entire time. I can only imagine the disaster that would have led to.

But if Dom didn't stick around to mess with Deacon, why didn't he follow me inside?

It was risky, I suppose. But he could have gone around to the front. Or slipped inside when Aaron wasn't looking.

My throat tightens.

Oh, my god. What is wrong with me? I don't care that he didn't bother to say bye. He's said he's coming back tonight. It's not a big deal.

"Thank you," I tell Deacon. Getting my mind back to where it needs to be. "You didn't have to do that—hangout with my brother—but... well, thanks." I'm sure Aaron appreciated the distraction as much as I did.

Deacon waves me off. "Don't sweat it. It's not like it was some hardship. He's a cool dude. Needs better taste in friends." He smirks. "But aside from that, he's an alright guy."

I throw my pillow at him. Deacon ducks to avoid it and throws an arm out at the same time, catching it in the air.

"Hey! What was that for?" he asks, but the twinkle in his eyes tells me he knows exactly what it was for.

"We have the same friends," I remind him.

"Your point?" He smirks, giving me a knowing look.

"Oh, yeah?" I chuck another pillow at his head. Knowing I'll miss, I follow it up with a third pillow, one that hits its mark, smacking him square in the face.

"*Umpf.*"

He tosses the offending pillow back with a laugh, narrowly missing me before calling out, "Foul."

"You can't call a foul in a pillow fight." What kind of shit is that?

"Hell yes, I can."

Deacon has two pillows to my one and holds one in each hand, a silent warning in his gaze. "Surrender?" he says, but judging by the grin on his face, he doesn't want me to.

A wry smile curls the corners of my mouth. I can't remember the last time I played around like this, let alone had an actual pillow fight. "Never."

Bouncing on the balls of my feet, I wait for his next move, but he surprises me.

Instead of throwing a pillow my way, Deacon charges across my room, holding the pillows out in front of his chest as he barrels into me like a sumo wrestler and shoves me back onto my bed. An unladylike squeal slips past my lips as I fly backwards, the soft mattress cushioning my fall.

Before I can catch my breath to retaliate, Deacon whacks me in the face with both pillows, one after the other, laughing the whole time.

"No fair!" I struggle to shove free from my cushion-filled cocoon, but he doesn't make it easy for me.

Deacon holds himself in check, keeping his hits playful while I swing at him with everything I've got. I'm a little competitive and he has an obvious advantage—his size, weight, and the fact that he has *two* pillows to my one.

Completely unfair.

"Last chance," he shouts over my shrieks. "Surrender now!"

We're both laughing so hard now that only one in five strikes connects. We look like a pair of toddlers without aim as we swing at one other between fits of laughter and, oh my god, I'm wheezing now.

"Ne—Nev—Never!" My voice breaks off in a squeal. I can hardly breathe. My chest heaves as I gasp between laughing and cursing, but I'm still going back for more.

Deciding on a Hail Mary, I throw my pillow one last time, missing him by a mile but using the distraction to lunge to the floor where I collapse, flat on my back, and admit defeat.

Deacon drops to the ground beside me, leaning against the side of my bed as he sits on the floor, elbows propped on his knees. "You're all fire, aren't you?" Sweat dots his brow, and he sucks in a lungful of air, as out of breath as I am.

"And a little brimstone," I say. "Or so I've been told."

He grins and I can't help but respond with a smile of my own. This is nice. Better than getting out of the house. Even better than Golden Tee.

"Today was—exactly what I needed. Thank you."

"You need to stop thanking me or it'll just go to my head.," he warns.

Rolling to my stomach, I tuck my hands beneath my chin and peer up at him. "You mean that giant ego of yours can get even bigger?"

"You're lucky I can't reach any of the pillows." He leans forward and ruffles my already messy hair. "But, I can do this."

"Hey!" I smack his hands away before pushing myself into a sitting position. "Rude," I snap, but with no actual heat in my voice.

He shrugs and leans back, giving me a peculiar look.

"Why are you being so nice to me?" I don't know what prompts me to voice the question out loud. Even to my own ears, it sounds stupid. But I have this nagging feeling, warning me this is too good to be true. That Deacon's friendship can't be this simple. Nothing ever is.

Besides, guys and girls are never really friends. Not in the strictly platonic—but we still hang-out, one-on-one—sense. Sure, I'm friends with Emilio and Roman, but through their girlfriends. Not because we have this close connection. I know they have my back, but even that is largely driven by their relationship with Aaron and has nothing to do with me directly. We all get along, but I couldn't see myself just kicking it with either of them the way I am with Deacon right now.

It'd be weird.

"Don't get me wrong," I rush to say. "I appreciate it. But I'm trying to wrap my head around why you'd even want to be friends with me after everything Dom's put you through. *Especially* after everything Dom's put you through."

His expression sobers, and he rubs the back of his neck, making the uncertain feeling I was just having bloom into something more. He searches for his words, which is both telling and incredibly frustrating. Like he has something to hide.

He shouldn't be trying to tell me what he thinks I want to hear. All I want is the truth. Too much in my life has gone to crap recently. And I don't want to rely on his friendship only to realize later on that it was all one-sided.

"I think ..." He hesitates before rolling his head on his shoulders and meeting my gaze. "We just vibe. Don't you think?"

He offers what is meant to be an easy smile, but the tick in his jaw gives way to the fact that it's forced.

"Yeah. We vibe. But there's more to it than that." I know I'm missing something here. Come on, Deacon. Don't prove me right. *Please.*

A multitude of emotions flicker across his face before he lets out a heavy sigh full of resignation. "Can I ask you one question first?"

"And then you'll answer mine?"

He nods. "Yes. I just... " Mashing his lips together, his nostrils flare before he forces out the question. "What do you see in Price?"

Brows drawn together, I close my eyes for a beat, letting his question settle over me. So, this is because of Dominique? Is he using me to get to him? Was that the goal this entire time?

Opening my eyes again, I try to shove down my disappointment, hanging on to one final shred of hope as I ask, "That's your question? Before you can tell me whether or not you have some ulterior motive for befriending me, you want to know what I see in Dominique Price?"

"Humor me."

I'd love to. Rolling my eyes, I pull my knees to my chest. "There isn't anything to see. We're friends..."

But, are we?

No.

We're really not.

"Or sorta friends. Maybe more like acquaintances who can be friendly to each other on occasion but prefer to go after one another's throats." I shrug. "I don't really know what we are to each other. How to label it. Frenemies is probably a better word but it sounds stupid." I'm rambling. I don't ramble often but when I do, nothing short of natural disaster can stop me.

"He and Aaron have been friends since high school. Well, on-again, off-again, friends. They're worse than a dating couple but for the last three years, they've been in the on-again stage. Things were murky before that."

I'm giving Deacon more information than he needs. Making the answer to his question infinitely more complicated. Forcing myself to pause in my mini rant, I suck in a lungful of air and try to catch my breath but since Deacon doesn't make any new comments, I pick up where I left off and prattle on some more.

"Since Aaron and Dominique are friends, it makes us friends by association. Neither of us really have a choice about that. We're in the same social circle so we're forced to see each other on a pretty regular basis. So yeah." I clap my hands together. "That's the deal with Dominique and me. We're not friends but we're also not enemies. We're this weird in between thing. I know I can count on him.. He's—" my lips curve downward into a frown, "been there for me with the shit I'm going through." All true but there's something about saying it out loud that shoots a shock of surprise through me. Dominique Price is there for me.

Who would have thought?

Maybe we are friends after all. My frown deepens. Could we be? Not in the *hey, let's hangout, share secrets, and be BFFs forever,* sort of way. But maybe in the *you drive me insane but you've got my back so I've got yours* kind of way.

Huh. I didn't realize until this moment that I've always felt like I can count on him.

"Friends by association?" He doesn't sound convinced.

"Yup." My explanation was clear as mud so I shouldn't be surprised by his confusion.

The ramble didn't help.

Deacon pushes his tongue to the inside of his cheek and gives a hard shake of his head. "Help me out here," he says. "You're not friends. But you're not enemies. You don't see anything in the guy or at least that's the impression you're trying to give me. And there's nothing particular about him that draws your attention? He's just one of your brother's friends?"

That sounds right so I give him a nod.

"But you're fucking him so ..." he trails off. "That's where I'm getting lost here."

I open my mouth to respond, before snapping it closed. Did he just—Am I—Oh Fuck.

"Umm... *Shit. Shit. Shit.*

Deacon holds up a hand. "Don't bother coming up with a lie," he says. "Price puts out some hardcore, '*stay the fuck away,*' and she '*belongs to me*' vibes." He makes air quotes around his words. "A guy like him doesn't do that with a chick he isn't sleeping with. So..."

"So..." I stretch out the word, buying myself a few extra seconds to formulate my response. "The *stay the fuck away* vibes are because he's protective. All the guys in our circle are like that. You know Roman Valdez and Emilio Chavez.

They're the same way because I'm Aaron's little sister." And since they participated in Dominique's shenanigans when he and the rest of the team were putting Deacon through the wringer for accidentally leaving a mark on my arm after we crashed into one another in the halls, it makes it believable.

"Don't read more into it than what's there."

Deacon gives me a *do I look stupid?* look, so I try again.

"And the *mine* shit." I shake my head. "You're seeing things that aren't there. Dominique has no claim on me."

"But he wishes he did."

I stifle a laugh. "No. He doesn't." Dom doesn't do relationships. "I'm just his friend's annoying little sister. You have sisters. I'm sure you know how it is."

Deacon's expression turns contemplative.

My stomach tightens as a sudden realization takes root. Deacon can use his suspicions against me. Against Dominique.

No matter how vigorously I deny them, and even without a single shred of proof, there is nothing to stop him from spreading his hunch around campus. All it would take are a few comments to his fraternity buddies and the rumor mill would take off like wildfire.

"You can't tell—"

Seeing the panicked look on my face, Deacon reaches out, resting his hand on my knee before giving it a comforting squeeze.

"Relax." He says. "You don't have anything to worry about. I won't tell anyone that you're *not* fucking Price." He rolls his eyes to the ceiling and shrugs. "Gossip isn't my thing. And I don't fuck over my friends"

He withdraws his touch, but despite his reassurance, alarm bells go off in my ears. Aaron cannot find out. Not from Deacon or anyone else. He'd confront Dominique about it if anyone so much as suggested we were involved with one another and while we agreed Aaron could never find out, I doubt Dom would lie to his face if he asked him directly.

Which means everything would be ruined.

"Because there's nothing to tell, right?" Please, say *right*. Agree with me and we can drop this entire thing. I won't even ask why you're my friend anymore.

Deacon ignores the silent plea in my gaze and shakes his head. "No. There is something to tell."

My eyes widen and my heart plummets to my feet.

"You and Price are screwing. Whether you admit to it or not is your problem, not mine. But only a blind person would miss the sexual tension between you two. Both of you are obvious as shit. But it's like I said. I don't do gossip. Your business is your own. And I don't fuck over my friends."

My breaths come fast, panic clawing up my throat and rendering me mute.

"You can relax." He shrugs his broad shoulders. "I only brought it up because I need to know how a girl like you winds up with a guy like him. I never took you for the type to be okay with being some jock's dirty little secret."

EIGHT
DOMINIQUE

The need to blow off some steam after seeing Kasey with Deacon damn near overwhelms me. Making the logical choice, I head for the gym. It's that or punch that fucker in the face, which will earn me a suspension in next week's game at best. I wouldn't put it past the fucker to rat me out. I'm surprised he still hasn't for the shit I put him through during practice. Regardless, resorting to violence is out of the question, no matter how appealing it sounds. So, the gym it is.

There's a large one on campus with state-of-the-art machines and equipment, but like most of the team, I prefer making use of the smaller one situated on the edge of campus. It's reserved for athletes, so I'm less likely to be bothered. Or at least, that's what I thought. But as soon as I step inside, I catch sight of Roman Valdez as he sits up at the incline bench.

Wiping the sweat from his face, he looks up and his dark brown eyes meet mine. Mouth pressed into a tight line, Roman gives me a look of concern. *Shit.* Coming here was a mistake.

"Hey man. Everything good?"

No way am I that fucking obvious.

With a grunt in response, I ignore his question and head for the free weights to pick up a set of dumbbells.

"Coach will have your ass if you fuck your shoulder up more than it already is," Roman warns, having followed me.

"I'm taking it easy," I grit out, not bothering to count my reps. This end of the gym is covered in wall to wall mirrors, so keeping my eyes trained forward, I track Roman as he grabs his own set of weights before taking up position beside me. Knew I couldn't get rid of him that easily.

We settle into a routine, neither of us talking as we work through our set. When my biceps begin to burn, I change things up, shifting my position. Bending at my knees, I hunch forward, careful to keep my back straight as I start up a set of tricep extensions that light the backs of my arms on fire, but this is a good kind of pain.

Roman does a few more curls before matching my stance and following my workout. He keeps his mouth closed, but knowing the broody fucker, the silence between us won't last.

After tricep curls, I move into lateral raises, gritting my teeth when my shoulder screams at me to stop. Fuck. This might be too much. I fight through the pain, ignoring the sweat dripping down my brow. I'm only five reps in when Roman drops his weight to the ground with a muttered curse.

With a furious glint in his eyes, he steps in front of me, arms folded and eyes narrowed as he stares down his nose at me.

"What the hell, man?" I ignore him and continue with my set. Only a few seconds pass before he curses again and makes to grab the dumbbells from my hands. Not putting up a fight, I let him have them and he drops them at our feet.

The weights hit the mat with a loud thud. I lift my gaze, meeting Roman's glare with one of my own.

"Do you mind?" I grind out.

His nostrils flare. "Yeah, *cabrón*. I mind. We have a game against PacNorth in less than two weeks and we need you if we're going to win."

Working my jaw, I lean forward to grab my weights, but Roman's hands on my chest shove me back.

"You. Dominique Price. The team needs you. Not Deacon Hunt. Where the hell is your head at?"

Fuck if I know. Leaving the weights where they are, I turn around and stalk off in the direction of the locker rooms, but of course Roman follows. Like a dog with a bone, that asshole never leaves well enough alone.

Stripping my shirt over my head, I turn and head for the showers, turning the water to cold. It's my third one of the day, but fuck if I care. Dropping the rest of my clothes, I step under the spray, hissing as the cold water sends needles of ice into my skin.

I make quick work of rinsing the sweat from my body despite the temptation to drag it out. A quick glance in Roman's direction shows he's got no problem waiting. A little nudity doesn't bother him.

Turning the water off, I grab one of the hanging towels and wrap it around my waist. I keep a few extra changes of clothes at the gym and head for my locker to retrieve one of them. Roman stays a few steps behind me like a wraith, forcing me to acknowledge his presence.

"My shoulder is better." Something he's aware of given he practices with me more days than not. "Stop with the hovering."

"Your shoulder is only fine because you've been taking it easy and using your other arm during practice, but with the weights you were lifting, it's almost like you want to re-injure your shoulder. Why?"

Shaking the water from my hair, I throw on my clothes, chewing over my response. "They were well under my max." It's not a lie.

"And well over the weight restriction the team doctor put you on." Also not a lie. "You've been careful for weeks. What the hell happened to make you suddenly lose so many brain cells you'd risk injury all over again? Are you trying to fuck what's left of our season?"

My jaw clenches and I hang my head, hearing the disappointment in his voice.

"No." I slam my locker shut and press my forehead against it. "I'm not looking to fuck up our season, okay? I just needed to blow off some steam."

"Why?" His expression is tight as he looks me over. He leans against the lockers, crossing his arms over his chest.

I want to tell him everything that's going on. The shit with Aaron. How I've been sleeping with Kasey. Everything. But none of it is my shit to tell, so instead of responding, I mirror his stance, folding my own arms over my chest.

"For once, Rome, can you let this one go?"

He gives me a look. One that gives me a loud and clear *no* in answer.

"Does this—"

"Price, you're here?" Coach walks in, drawing both our attention. "Good," he continues as though I responded. "I need a word." He flicks his head toward Roman. "Valdez," he greets.

Roman nods.

Coach turns his attention back to me, dismissing Roman from the conversation. "In private," he adds and then stalks off to the office he keeps in the back.

Exhaling a breath of relief, I follow him. With any luck, Roman will be gone by the time Coach finishes filling me in on whatever it is that's on his mind.

Coach takes a seat behind his desk while I move in to claim one of the two positioned on the opposite side from him. Tugging back the worn fabric covered chair, I sink onto the nearly nonexistent cushion and lean forward, threading my fingers together and resting my elbows on my knees.

Coach cuts right to the chase. "I got a call early this morning." He gives me a knowing look like I should know what the call was about, only I haven't got a clue as to what he's talking about. When it becomes obvious that I'm in the dark here, he leans back in his seat and gives me an assessing look.

"An agent for the Richland Royals reached out to me." An agent for the—no shit! It takes several beats for his words to hit me. "He wants to set up a meeting between you and Andres DeAnde."

If I hadn't grown up with nannies and tutors who constantly preached the laws of etiquette while growing up, my jaw would be open and on the floor. But regardless of my upbringing, I'm struggling to maintain my composure. To hold onto my usual mask of indifference. This is big. And completely out of left field.

"What does the owner of the Richland Royals want with me?" I've never met the guy. Not that I'm suggesting I should have.

DeAnde is an NFL team owner and I'm a college quarterback so far beneath him, it is shocking to know I've somehow caught his attention. If it wasn't for the football connection, I'd assume his interest had something to do with my parents. Richard and Sheridan Price have made it a habit to meddle in my life whenever it suits them. Scheduling interviews with tech executives, arranging dates with women they deemed suitable for marriage. It's never ending with the two of them.

But the one thing in my life my parents have never had an interest in, is football. There's no reason for them to call in any favors now. Not when they're the ones who've vehemently forbidden me from playing pro after graduation and going all the way.

"Good. You know who he is. Means you understand the seriousness of this." Coach leans forward in his seat and steeples his fingers on top of the desk. "I have no idea what he wants from you. And before you say what I think you're about to, give this opportunity some thought. You don't have to give me an answer right now, but I'm willing to hear one if—"

He holds up a finger when I open my mouth to respond, and I bite back my words, snapping my mouth shut to wait until he's finished.

"I'm willing to hear your answer now if and only if the answer you give me is a yes. If you want to say anything besides that, I want you to sleep on it and come back to my office tomorrow."

Shaking my head, I bite back my curse. *Figures.* A weight of helplessness settles over my shoulders. It's a feeling I both hate and have grown accustomed to.

Coach knows I can't go down this road. Going pro isn't an option for me. It never has been. Never will be. I love the game. Would kill to go all the way and play professional. But playing professional football has never been in the cards. My family won't allow it.

I drop my head into my hands. "Coach—"

"There's no harm in hearing the man out," he says, cutting me off. "It's a conversation. Doesn't have to be anything more. It'll take an hour of your time and you'll get a free meal out of it and yes. I know your family has more money than any one of you all can spend in a lifetime. You can buy your damn own meals." He huffs. "But, son..." He waits until I lift my head and meet his gaze. "You've got a real shot at making something of yourself and going into the big leagues. A year early, no less. An opportunity like this only comes around once in a lifetime. For most, it doesn't come around at all. Don't throw away this chance at the future *you* dream about over the misguided belief of family obligations. You follow the path that fits you." He stabs a finger at me from across the desk, his eyes full of expectation. "Not the one your parents laid out for you."

Clenching my fists, I expel a ragged breath, allowing a kernel of hope to unfurl inside my chest. *Fuck.* I can't believe I'm considering this.

Hope is a dangerous thing to have for someone like me. I thought I'd given up any semblance of the word years ago, but sitting here now ... *Shit.*

I want to do what Coach is suggesting. Follow my own path. Chase my own dreams. I want to believe I have that option. But—Fuck it.

"A conversation."

"Just a conversation," he confirms.

"When?" My parents know my comings and goings. They take overbearing parents to the extreme, and while Coach may think there is no harm in a sit down with the owner of the Richland Royals, there is if my parents catch wind of it.

I negotiated a deal with them back when I was a freshman in high school. One I know they have every intention of holding me to.

If they had it their way, I'd have gone to Suncrest Academy for high school before transferring to one of the few HBCUs —historically black colleges and universities. It's the path my younger sister is taking and the one I've fought like hell to avoid.

Freshman year, I made the case that Sun Valley High had a stronger football team than Suncrest Academy. A weak argument in their eyes given that the two ways of earning a living they vehemently despise for any young black man, let alone their son, is playing ball or making music.

According to my father, no son of his will stoop to the American stereotype of what makes a successful black man. We are better than ballers and rappers, and he did not build a name for himself as one of the country's wealthiest men—not *black men*—but one of the wealthiest *men* in the nation, just to see his flesh and blood throw his legacy away to do something as insignificant as playing a game.

I made the argument nonetheless, reminding him that to be the best, you had to play and win against the best. Football might hold no value in his eyes, but I refused to play on a mediocre team. I would excel in everything I did. Including football. I even put together a speech detailing how playing football in high school was a strategic move on my part that directly benefited my future, explaining how it placed me in a position of power within our community.

Being a football player wouldn't just make me popular. It'd make me revered. And not only by my fellow classmates but also by the school faculty and administrative staff. It'd also increase my profile and status with members of our community. People would come to recognize me and my name.

And they did.

Because after weeks of arguing my case, my father relented and gave me the green light to enroll at Sun Valley High. At the time, winning an argument against Richard Price was the biggest achievement of my life. And I was damn proud of myself.

Junior year when my father started talking about colleges, I made the same case.

And failed. Miserably.

To my father, there was no point in playing college ball when my time was better spent on my studies and learning more about the family business—Peretti and Price, a multi-billion dollar tech company.

Yes. Billion with a B.

Coach wasn't exaggerating when he said my family has more money than they can spend in a lifetime. With money comes power, entitlement, and an overwhelming belief that you are always right.

My father has all three of these and he does a good job at surrounding himself with people who are too afraid to ever tell him he is wrong.

Thankfully, I'm not one of those people.

Things got heated and there were pockets of time where we refused to speak to each other.

The problem with my family that is unique from others, is that my parents have both the power and the financial means to back up any threat they make.

My father swore he would never let me play football in college. And I believed him.

My sister, Monique, took dance classes behind his back when we were in high school—another activity my parents detest, claiming no daughter of theirs would become some backup hussy for music videos—which is beside the point.

Mo was fifteen and wanted to take hip-hop classes to spend more time with her friends. She wasn't out there shaking her ass for money or putting on some sleazy number with aspirations of dancing in some black light music video. Not that her intentions mattered. As he does with most things, our father turned her ambitions for dance into something it wasn't.

When he found out she'd gone behind his back and enrolled for classes after he'd explicitly told her no, he had his assistant call every studio within a one-hundred-mile radius and had her blacklisted.

Then he made a personal call to the headmaster at Suncrest Academy and had his own daughter removed from the school dance team. Indefinitely.

Monique was heartbroken.

It wasn't the first time I saw him throw his weight around to get what he wanted. But, it was the first time he'd directed his attention toward one of his own children in such a brutal and demoralizing way.

I learned then and there that mine and my sister's happiness meant nothing to our parents. They cared about appearances and legacy and would let nothing get in the way of the future they'd mapped out for us.

The lesson stuck.

But if I've inherited any traits from my father, it is my sheer stubbornness. After seeing what he did to Monique, I knew when it came to me, there could be no half measures.

He insisted I go to an HBCU.

I applied for nothing but state schools.

He refused to let me play college football.

I refused to go to college at all.

I reached the point where I'd spit in my own face just to spite him.

He thought I'd fold, but I didn't. Like Mount Saint Helens in the spring of 1980, I was an immovable mountain simmering on the edge of explosion.

The more my father pushed, the harder I pushed back.

I was strategic in my rebellion. Every move I made across the chess board of our relationship put me one step closer to getting what I wanted. I weighed each argument. Calculated the risks.

My boldest rebellion was when I sent letters of regret to every single HBCU he submitted an application of admittance on my behalf to. To this day, I've never seen him so enraged as he was when he found out. But by then, he'd already refused me the one thing I wanted. There was nothing he could take from me that would bring me to heel.

We fought on and off about college my entire junior year of high school and most of my senior year. The battle was hard fought. And my reward was well earned.

After eighteen months of brutal back and forth, he buckled and agreed to let me play ball, but under two conditions. The first was that unless I agreed to attend an HBCU, I'd have to pay my own way through college. I'd have zero access to my parents' money and I was on my own not only for tuition but also for housing, food, and all of my basic necessities. The only financial asset he couldn't withhold from me was my Escalade. I'd already paid it off and had the registration transferred into my name the day after I turned eighteen.

My father assumed I'd balk at the prospect of footing my own bills. I didn't. I was a straight A student and the star quarterback for my school earning me a full ride scholarship to play at Suncrest U—my number one choice.

My father has never understood the fact that I don't want or need his money. Having a loaded bank account is not a motivating factor for me. He should have seen that when I picked an Escalade as my first car after I turned fifteen.

He gave me the choice of anything I wanted which included rides like a Drako GTE and Bentley Bacalar. There was no budget. No price tag he'd consider too high. Yet of all the luxury cars I could have picked from, I settled on a Cadillac fucking Escalade.

It was a fraction of the price coming in at seventy-seven thousand and most importantly, it was something I could pay off and own. Something that'd be mine entirely.

The second condition my father insisted on was my agreement to walk away from football once I graduated college. I'd expected it but it didn't make it any easier of a pill to swallow.

I knew Football would never be my future. But I won four more years to play, so long as I agreed to take my rightful place at my father's side and step into the family business when the time came.

I took the deal.

There was no alternative that granted me the ability to play. And I've spent the past three years resigned to the fact that going pro is nothing but a pipe dream.

And Coach wants me now to believe I have a shot? That having something as mundane as a conversation with one man can somehow make a difference?

"Next Sunday afternoon. Your meeting with Andres DeAnde will be after Saturday's game. You stay one extra night and we play it off to the rest of the team that you're taking a day to rest. Maybe seeing a specialist about your shoulder. No one needs to be the wiser."

Before I can stop myself, I nod. "Okay." I'm going to regret this.

"Glad to hear it. You're making the right choice, son."

"You know nothing will come out of this."

We both rise to our feet. Coach holds out a hand to me, and I reach forward to shake it.

"You'll be surprised to know not everyone is afraid to go up against a Price." He winks. "Some people might even look forward to it."

"What's that supposed to mean?" Rocking back on my heels, I parse out his words, searching for some hidden meaning.

"You'll see." With only a vague response, he ushers me out of his office and steers me out the door. "It's getting late. Go, rest up." I glance at the clock as I leave, taking note of the time.

It's a little after six.

Roman waits for me in the locker room, likely already sorting his thoughts for my impending interrogation. Swallowing down a frustrated groan I jerk my head to the door in silent question. *You coming?*

I'm meeting up with Aaron for dinner. Might as well bring Roman's ass along so he can poke at Henderson and forget about whatever questions he has sitting on the tip of his tongue for me.

"I am not anyone's dirty little secret," I snap. Eyes wide, I jerk both of my hands to my face, covering my mouth as I immediately catch my mistake. *Dammit*. My reaction does nothing to prove my own point. If anything, it only serves to confirm his.

"*Right.*" Deacon gives me a knowing look. "You're cool with Price hiding the fact the two of you are boning while he struts around campus as a free agent, enjoying all the perks that come along with being a division one athlete and unattached. You have no problem with the endless line of women who throw themselves at him every chance they get. I have a hard time believing that, Kasey."

Well, not when he puts it like that. Obviously I'm not okay with women throwing themselves at him. Not because he's mine or anything. But we have an arrangement. One I suggested which means I am not his dirty little secret. If anything, Dominique Price is mine.

"Can you honestly sit there and tell me you're okay with letting Price have his cake and eat it too?"

"You misunderstood." I aim for flippancy, but my attempt at a *zero fucks to give* attitude falls flat on the mattress between us.

This is harder than I thought it'd be. But if I can't convince Deacon that there's nothing going on between Dom and I, what hope do I have if the time comes when I have to deny what I'm doing to my friends, or worse, my brother?

"I meant I'm not his dirty secret because we aren't sleeping together. Therefore, there's no secret to keep." I wave a dismissive hand in the air.

My denial falls on deaf ears.

"He's using you. You know that, right? Whatever lies Price is telling you, that's all they are. Lies. He won't settle down with you. He won't offer you a real or meaningful relationship. The kind you deserve. He's not capable of it. There is no happy ending where Dominique Price is concerned."

Deacon's earlier playfulness is gone, leaving behind an edge of steel in his voice.

My first impulse is to reject his words. He doesn't know what he's talking about. Deacon's been on the team with Dominique for a handful of months. Hardly enough time to get to know someone let alone get a sense of their character.

A spark ignites deep inside me, demanding Deacon admit that he's wrong. I want him to take back his words. To eat each and every one of them until there is zero risk of him spewing them back out.

The urge to defend Dominique is overwhelming.

But a single question filters through my mind. *Why should I care?* We aren't in a relationship and neither one of us wants one. Not with each other.

Dominique isn't denying me some fairytale romance I secretly want. He's not lying to me or manipulating my feelings. He's playing by *my* rules. Which makes Deacon's assumptions irrelevant.

"Be honest, if not with me, then with yourself. Are you really okay being the side chick Price keeps tucked away? The one he brings out when he wants an easy lay? That's not you, Kasey. You're better than that."

"Way to deliver that backhanded compliment. Asshole," I snap. "Let's set the misogyny aside for the rest of the day. And for the last time, there is no me and Dominique."

"Stop with the bullshit." He rubs his temples. "You're giving me a headache. I know you and Price are sleeping together. Stop denying it."

Anxious energy scales up my chest and into my throat. My jaw tightens hard enough for me to hear my teeth grind down on each other.

Let. It. Go.

"I'm trying to look out for you," he adds. "I don't want to see you get hurt."

"You're looking out for me by calling me someone's side-chick while attempting slut shaming me?"

"What? Fuck. No. That's not what I'm doing at all." He throws his head back, eyes cast up at the ceiling. "I'm not slut shaming you."

Dropping his head back down, his honey gold eyes meet mine. "I swear, and if you took it that way, I'm sorry. I'm not judging you or your decisions. Okay?"

Teeth pressed together I nod for him to continue but agreeing to hear him out doesn't mean I'm going to forget what he said.

Deacon scrubs both hands over his face, exhaustion tugging at his features.

"Dominique Price comes from a prominent black family."

"I'm aware," I deadpan.

Everyone in Sun Valley knows who the Price family is. They founded one of the largest tech companies in the country. They're like Bill Gates, but bigger. More prestigious. Hence Dominique's oversized ego. Though based on this conversation, I'd bet Deacon can give him a run for his money in the arrogance department.

Deacon's gaze sweeps over me all the way from my bare feet to my unruly hair and freckled nose. He scrutinizes my appearance before exhaling a harsh breath and shaking his head. "I don't think you are. Because if you were, you'd know there's a stigma in the black community. One that directly relates to women like you" he says.

"What do you mean women like me?"

"There's this belief that white women—like yourself—steal all of the quote-unquote *good black men.*"

My nose wrinkles at his words. "That's stupid."

"No. It's reality."

Yeah, no. I'm not buying it. "And you're telling me all this because—" Get to the point, Deacon. I don't have all day and my patience is already thin.

"Price will never date, let alone marry, a white woman. Not publicly and not in any sort of meaningful way. His family and his upbringing would never allow it. He'll fuck you in secret behind closed doors but you'll never get anything more than that. He'll never offer what a girl like you deserves."

I rear back as if struck. "Wow." I mean, I'm not trying to be the girl he settles down with, but hearing it said like that, it stings.

Mouth pinched into a tight line, I look away. I'm not so naïve as to believe race doesn't matter to people. But Dom has not once ever treated me any different because I'm white. And I sure as hell have never treated him differently for being black.

The color of our skin never mattered.

Sun Valley is a melting pot. If anything, it's me who is in the minority. We're a largely Hispanic community with a decent percentage of Asian and African cultures making Deacon's words an even harder pill to swallow.

But there's an echo of truth in what he has to say. I remember years back having a conversation with Monique— Dominique's sister.

She'd been dating this guy all through her senior year and before graduation, she decided to take him home for one of her family's weekly Sunday dinners. It was meant to be a surprise because things were getting serious enough between the two of them that she wanted to introduce him to her parents.

She was so excited.

Only, things didn't go as planned and they wound up breaking things off the very next day. She cried about it. A lot. And despite claims that it was for the better, I never really understood. When I asked her about the break up, she said their cultures were incompatible. Long term, it would never work out and it was better to end things now before it got more complicated.

Only a few weeks earlier she talked about how they planned to make their relationship work when they were away at college. They'd be at different schools but in the same state, and Monique had it all planned out.

They both did.

I didn't know Yuze well, but the few times I met him, he doted on her. He never shied away from showing his affection or telling her with words how much she mattered. It's one of the things Monique loved most about him. His capacity to love.

When I reminded her of that, she doubled down. She was black and Yuze was Japanese. *It could never work.*

I let it go.

I'm white and very much Americanized. I can't claim to understand the type of cultural differences they'd face as a multicultural couple.

Mom is German. Fourth generation in the United States. Her family immigrated to the states after World War II when it wasn't a proud time to be German. The way she explains it, her great-grandparents were desperate to fit in and acclimate to their new home. The German language was forbidden from being spoken in their household and they refused to celebrate any traditionally German holidays. They were ashamed of the country they came from and did everything they could to repress their culture, stripping it not only from their generation but from the generations of family members to come.

Over time, I'm told things got better. By the time my grandmother was born, the family integrated back some of their traditions. They lost a lot of their roots; but they were able to reclaim some of the more nostalgic things they carried fond memories of, like particular foods and celebrations.

But then the Dust Bowl hit. My mom's family originally settled in Oklahoma when they immigrated to the states and between dust storms, drought, and the great depression, they had to migrate halfway across the country and, not for the first time, faced pressure to assimilate.

Californians didn't appreciate refugee farm families migrating into the area. Mom told me stories her grandmother once told her. How people would call Great Gram an *Okie* like it was a dirty word and something she should be ashamed of when neither she nor any of the other tens of thousands of people forced to leave their homes could have controlled what happened back in Oklahoma.

The move forced them to give up pieces of themselves all over again.

By the time Aaron and I were born, there was almost nothing left. When Mom and Dad were still married, we'd celebrate *Weihnachtstag*—German Christmas. And she'd make us german pancakes with powdered sugar and lemon curd for breakfast.

If Mom was feeling particularly nostalgic, she'd make *Kartoffelkloesse* as a treat to go with dinner later on in the day. They were these weird potato dumplings fried in butter. Back then, I hated them. I never understood the appeal. They were these balls of mush and when I say she fried them, don't imagine a deep fried crust or anything like that. There was no shell that would form, giving the dumplings any sort of crunch or texture. They were just buttery mush.

But I'd give anything for a plate of those ugly beige baseball sized things. Closing my eyes, I try to picture Mom in the kitchen with her apron dusted in flour and her hair tied up in a mess.

Tears burn the backs of my closed lids.

Don't think about that, I order myself. *Don't think about her.*

But as I struggle not to recall memories of my mother, I realize it's harder now than it was to picture her face. The way she smelled. The sound of her laugh.

A silent sob wracks my body. Desperately, I shove the ball of grief climbing up my throat away.

Blinking hard, I refocus my gaze on Deacon, reminding myself of his words as I backtrack through my thoughts and give myself the precious seconds needed to get my emotions back under control.

Rubbing at the dull ache between my breasts with the heel of one hand, I use the other to pull out my phone and thumb through the contacts illuminated on the screen.

Deacon's opinions aren't enough to convince me. But someone else's might tip the scales.

Despite what some people may think, race and culture are wildly different things. Yuze and Monique breaking up over cultural differences would center around the cultural expectations each of them has for living their lives.

The holidays they celebrate. The way they want to raise their children. Their system of beliefs. Their values. It encompasses norms, or unwritten rules, that are simple like never wearing shoes in the house, all the way up to more complex expectations like gender roles in the relationship or what religion to practice and impart on their children.

Race is separate from culture. It refers to outward, physical characteristics. The most common being the color of your skin but it also includes features like the shape of your eyes, the fullness of your lips, and the strength of your jaw.

I could see Yuze and Monique's cultures being different but he didn't strike me as the sort of guy who'd reject Monique's traditions in favor of his own. If what Deacon suggests is true, and it's a big if, then race could have played a part in Mo's relationship too.

You can merge cultures and find a balance. But there is no compromise in race. You can't ask someone to change their appearance let alone the color of their skin.

Finding her name in my contacts list, I start a new message and my fingers fly over the screen.

Me: Couple years back when you and Yuze broke up, was it because he was Japanese and you're black?

THE COLOR of the message bubble changes and the word *read* pops up beneath my text on the screen. Holding my breath, I watch for the three little dots to appear, indicating that she's typing out a response.

Bingo.

"Who are you—"

I hold up one hand. "Give me a second."

Monique: Sorta. There were other reasons, too, but it was part of it. My parents flipped out when they realized he wasn't black. Why?

MY SKIN LEECHES OF COLOR. There's my confirmation. Swallowing hard, I type out a quick response.

Me: No reason. Random thought. Thanks.

TOSSING my phone to my bed, I slump down onto the floor.

"Did you get what you need?" Deacon asks.

I guess I did.

Twisting the hair tie around my wrist, I struggle to come to terms with the realization that race matters to Dominique Price.

Whatever he thinks or however he feels about me and if I'm happily ever after material or not should make no difference to me. Not when I've said again and again that this is sex. Nothing more. And nothing less.

So why is this new knowledge tearing a hole in my chest, eviscerating my heart, and leaving behind a gaping wound of realization that we will never be anything more than fuck buddies.

"I'm sorry." Sympathy weighs heavy in his voice. "I didn't tell you this to hurt you."

"You didn't." I force the brittle words past my lips and give him a self deprecating smile before taking in a deep breath and squaring my shoulders.

None of this can touch me unless I allow it to.

"Dominique will marry some respectable black woman one day and live happily ever after. The end. I don't see what that has to do with me."

Deacon's expression softens, and he leans forward, tracing the line of my jaw with his calloused thumb.

"More lies." His tone is laced with resignation. "But I get it. You don't trust me," he says the words casually, giving nothing of his thoughts away.

I get the feeling he wants me to deny his statement. To assure him that I do trust him. Only, I don't. Deacon hasn't been in my life long enough for us to develop that level of trust.

"Sorry." My mouth twists into a grimace. "I should have believed you but I needed Monique to confirm it." Lifting both shoulders, I shrug. What more is there to say?

Picking at a stray piece of lint on my pants, I worry my lower lip and wait to see what he says but when the room remains quiet save for the sound of our breaths, I decide to circle back to where our conversation started now that he's made his point.

"You asked your question and I answered. But you've still yet to answer mine."

"Fair enough." Deacon drops his hand from my face. "Let's make a deal. I show you my hand. You show me yours. Agreed?" He gives me an expectant look.

"Didn't I already show you mine?" I ask.

He quirks a brow, the glint in his eyes mocking.

"No. Unless you're admitting now to sleeping with Price.

Whatever.

Rolling my eyes I fold my arms over my chest and level Deacon with an exasperated glare.

My irritation bounces off of him like a taut rubber band leaving him wholly unfazed.

"Remind me what it is I get out of doing this?"

The corners of his mouth twist into a wry grin, and some of the usually carefree expression I've come to associate with him bleeds back into his gaze.

"I want to be your friend—" I open my mouth to remind him we are friends, but Deacon doesn't pause long enough for me to get a word in. "A real friend. The kind you confide in. Can rely on. The type of friend that is more family than friend. I don't have that with anyone else, and I want it with you."

"Platonic friends?" I ask.

We have to be on the same page here. Deacon is attractive, don't get me wrong. And there are plenty of girls on campus who consider him the catch of a lifetime, but I'm not interested in him romantically and I won't lead him on.

Regret flashes over his face before he's able to mask it.

Squirming in my seat, I try and fail to ignore the spear of discomfort that worms inside me at that momentary display of emotion.

With a small smile that doesn't reach all the way to his eyes, Deacon inclines his head and with a dejected voice says, "If that's what you want, then yes. Strictly platonic."

Not the enthusiastic agreement I was hoping for but it'll do.

"Friends don't stab one another in the back," I say. "They don't hurt each other." I'm friendly with a lot of people but there are very few I genuinely count as friends. If he wants to be one of them, he'll need to know what I expect.

"I won't do anything to harm you. Not knowingly or willingly at least."

"You'll swear to that?"

He lifts one brow in question. "Like a pinky swear?" I'm almost surprised at the question but then I remember he's mentioned having younger sisters. A pinky swear is likely right up his alley.

"Yes. Exactly like a pinky swear."

Honey-colored eyes spark with amusement.

Shifting forward, I hold out my hand, pinky raised in the air. Giving him an expectant look, I wait for him to take it and after only a few seconds, he shakes his head with a soft chuckle and wraps his pinky finger around mine, giving it a firm shake.

"Cross my heart and hope to die."

His smile widens and he picks up the words for our promise. "Stick a needle in my eye."

"A secret is a secret. My word is forever."

"A promise between friends," he adds.

"Forever and ever," I finish the rhyme and release his pink.

"Happy now?" he asks.

"Yes. Thank you."

Shaking his head, he settles back against the bed and folds his hands behind his head.

"So, cards on the table?"

I nod. He pinky swore, and he knew the promise poem. I have no choice but to trust him now.

"At first, I didn't want to be your friend. I wanted in your pants."

He laughs at my dumbfounded expression and I swat him in the chest with the back of my hand.

"Don't look so surprised. You're hot. You can't blame a guy for trying"

Guys don't usually refer to me as hot. I've been told I'm pretty plenty of times growing up, but more often than not, I'm referred to as cute or, *gag,* adorable.

At just over five feet tall with a heart-shaped face, blue eyes, and loose, curly blond hair, I can't tell you the number of times people have joked that I'm cute and *fun sized.* Which for the record is not a compliment.

So hot? That's a new one for me.

"Um. Thanks."

"You're welcome." He lifts one shoulder in a small shrug. "But the same day we met is the same day Price decided I was enemy number one and after that..." He trails off.

I wait. *After that, what?* I want to question him but instead keep my mouth shut, giving him time to sort through his thoughts.

Deacon shifts on the floor, his expression growing decidedly uncomfortable. He coughs to clear his throat and flicks his gaze around my room, taking everything in as though he hasn't seen it already. His efforts to keep his gaze pointedly off of me aren't unnoticed.

"When I realized Price had a vested interest in you, and after I got over the beating I took everyday on the field, I may have allowed my animosity for him to steer my attention decisively your way."

"Why?" What is his problem with Dominique? Is it because he's the starting quarterback and Deacon is second string? He's an incoming freshman. Surely someone explained he has to work his way up in the team lineup? You can't expect to be MVP on day one.

"It's complicated," he hedges.

Yeah, that dodgy behavior isn't going to work. Deacon won't let me skirt around my truth. No way does he get to skirt around his own.

"Try me."

He exhales a loud breath before licking his lips. "Friends don't backstab. They don't share each other's secrets." He throws my words back at me.

"We pinky-swore," I remind him.

"This is one of those things you're going to want to tell people about but you can't. Not for any reason. Alright?"

"Unless you murdered someone and are about to tell me the coordinates for the body, we're good. I won't share your secrets." I make a gesture of zipping my mouth closed and tossing away an invisible key.

With a deep breath, Deacon shifts to face me again, his eyes holding my own, as he says six words I never would have expected to hear today.

"Dominique Price is my half brother."

TEN
KASEY

Dominique's dad is a dick. For the next half hour, I quietly sit and stare with what I'm sure is a dumbfounded look on my face, listening as Deacon explains how Dominique Price, of all people, is his half brother.

It's a sordid tale. I wish I was making it up. The manipulative bullshit his father put Deacon's mom through.

Richard Price had an affair with his then secretary—Victoria Hunt.

The relationship lasted over a year. He used his position of power as an authority figure to worm his way into her good graces. Then he manipulated the impressionable girl she was back then, leading her on and making her believe he loved her with promises to leave his wife so they could start a new life together, just the two of them.

She was young and naïve and he was ten years her senior. He painted her a picture-perfect fairytale.

"When she'd get restless," Deacon adds, "He'd always reassure her, telling her things like *'the only reason I haven't filed for divorce is because I need time to get my affairs in order.'*" His lip curls in disgust. "He told my mom his marriage was over and he begged her to be patient with him. To give him time. And she did. The way mom tells it, he'd break down, eyes glassy and face twisted with fear anytime he thought she was going to walk away. He was so convincing."

I place my hand on his arm and give it a squeeze. It's obvious this is hard for him.

"She believed him when he said he was afraid he'd lose his business—which even back then was already a million dollar organization—as a part of a settlement to his divorce. Sounds legit, right? And she believed him when he'd say he couldn't lose her. That he loved her."

God. What a bastard.

"She comforted him when he told her his biggest fear was that his wife would keep their son from him after he left her." He barks out a humorless laugh. "What a joke. You know, she thought he was a great dad back then. Thought he'd be a terrific father when the two of them had kids of their own."

Hanging his head, he shakes it. "When she found out she was pregnant," he says, "she was excited. She was only twenty-one, but she was excited to have me. I wasn't some burden or mistake to her. Not ever."

My heart clenches. The way he talks about her, it's clear they're close. Emotion clogs my throat and memories of my mom come to the surface before I shove them away. This isn't about me. It's about him.

"What happened?" I ask, knowing he needs to get this all out. How long has he been keeping this to himself? Protecting this secret? Deep down, I know what happened. Dominique doesn't know he has a half brother. If he did, I'd have heard about it. Which means, Richard Price chose not to play a role in Deacon's life. He might have contributed half of Deacon's DNA, but he didn't father him.

"What you can probably guess." His shoulders slump forward. Right now, he looks like a lost and confused little boy, and seeing him like this breaks my heart. Scooting closer, I lean my head on his shoulder, offering what little comfort I have to give. I can't relate to what he's feeling right now. Mom wanted to be there. She might not have known how to be a mom, trying too hard to be my friend instead of my parent, but she never once rejected me.

Dad has his own issues, too. But he's around and he helps, in his own way. Not always in the way I need. He likes to throw money at Aaron and me to get us to go away, but it's also how he shows his love. Every financial need of ours is met. Every opportunity is available to us. There's no warmth or comfort with my father. I can't remember the last time he hugged me or offered me any molecule of affection, but that's just how he is. Cold. Distant. But never indifferent.

"When she told him the good news, he lost it and demanded she get an abortion. She refused."

I suck in a breath and grimace. Good for her. Ending a pregnancy is a personal choice. No man gets to dictate that decision. Knowing Richard Price tried to pressure her into getting one makes me dislike the man even more.

"He threatened to leave her, but by then, the writing was on the wall." He shrugs. "She wasn't surprised when less than a week later, Peretti and Price let her go and terminated her position as his secretary. They gave her a severance package—fifty grand."

I whistle.

"Yeah. Equal to her yearly salary at the time."

"Hush money?" Fifty-grand isn't life changing money, but it is still a lot. And given that she was young — if it were me, even growing up with money, I probably would have taken it.

Deacon nods. "Yeah. To a twenty-one-year-old kid who grew up poor, it was a lot of money. More than she'd ever seen.." He shakes his head. "But kids are expensive and when you don't have a job and the medical bills pile up between checkups and ultrasounds and shit, you burn through your bank account a lot faster than you think."

"He didn't help after that?" The fifty grand should have been just the start of it.

He shakes his head. "Not a dime. She did it all on her own."

"Why didn't she fight him on it?" I ask. "She could have sued for child support. Forced him to help her. To support you." Dad paid child support for both Aaron and me, and not once that I've heard of did he ever fight Mom on it. Even after Aaron turned eighteen, he still paid his part, helping Aaron with tuition and with competition fees before Aaron picked up sponsors for boarding. He made a donation to Kappa Mu to secure my spot in the sorority. Footed the bill for my car so I could get around easier on campus. My dad is well off, but it's a drop in the bucket compared to the kind of money Dom's dad has at his disposal.

"Why would she?" His tone is dejected. "After I was born, she reached out. She messaged him a picture of me and asked if he wanted to meet me, and you know what he said?"

A gnawing sort of dread fills me.

"He told her he'd never fathered a half-breed bastard and that unless she wanted to find herself in court for defamation, he suggested she lose his number and never bother him again."

I gasp.

"That's what I am to him," he says. "A half-breed." His voice cracks on the word and I have to blink back the moisture in my eyes. Hurt ripples out from Deacon in invisible waves, and I wish I could help.

"Do you get it now?" he asks. "Appearances are everything to that family, and hell will freeze over before they allow a white woman into the fold." He gives me a sobering look. "And any child of yours would be a half-breed bastard like me, too."

Unwanted. Rejected. Ignored. He doesn't say those words out loud but they hang in the air between us, sinking poisonous claws of doubt into me.

Deacon leaves after that and for the next hour, I play his words back in my head. What Richard Price did to Deacon's mom is bullshit. But Dominique and I aren't in a relationship. We have no secrets or lies. Not between us, anyway. Or at least there weren't until Deacon spilled his.

Shit. I can't tell Dominique about this. *Double shit.*

Throwing myself back on my bed, I release a frustrated groan.

I don't owe Dominique anything. Not my secrets and certainly not Deacon's. But even at our worst, when our dislike for one another borders on hate, the loyalty we share has not once wavered. And keeping this from him, already it feels like a betrayal.

"Why did he—" My bedroom door swings open, and I cut off the rest of my words.

"Why did he, what?" A deep and familiar voice asks, sending a shiver of nervous energy down my spine.

Bolting up from my bed, I pat down my riot of curls in a vain attempt to tame my hair.

"What are you doing here?" It's the first thing that pops into my head, and judging by the displeased look on his face, it's the wrong question to ask.

Whoops.

He's here to punish me. Right. I may have looked forward to this whole punishment thing before, I'm definitely not looking forward to it now. I have too much on my mind. Too many scenarios playing out in my head.

Dominique's eyes drink me in and his already brooding expression darkens only this time, his dark brown eyes are flecked with heat, his heavy lidded gaze laced with desire.

He closes the door behind him. The snick loud in the quiet room. Dominique hesitates with his hand hovering over the door handle before flicking the lock and ensuring no unexpected visitors can come in. His long legs eat up the distance between us and he uses his broad shoulders and sheer size to crowd me back onto my bed.

"You know why I'm here." His chest vibrates with each one of his words, eliciting a small shiver beneath my skin.

I don't move as he lifts one hand, casually tracing the line of my jaw before cupping my cheek in his warm, calloused hand.

Eyes boring into mine, he strokes his thumb over my bottom lip. On instinct, my lips part and my tongue peeks out to taste the pad of his finger.

A growl of approval works its way up his throat and his eyes flood with a feral sort of need. The unmasked emotion is stark in its intensity as his gaze hones in on my mouth.

Tension builds between us, blanketing the air with the promise of pleasure.

"It's late. I didn't think you'd show." Any previous thoughts I had before evaporate when Dominique shifts his grip to the back of my neck, holding me captive before leaning in to capture my mouth in a bruising kiss.

There's no build up to what he's doing here and I imagine he's kissing me now the way he plans to fuck me later. Hard. Rough. Filled with his dominance and a desperate need to force me into submission.

I give into the promise on his lips, fisting my hands into the material of his shirt and yanking him closer. *Take me.* My actions all but demand.

He stumbles forward onto the bed but catches himself with his forearms on either side of me, keeping his weight from crushing me while he positions himself between my thighs.

Dominique adjusts our new position, lining up his already hard length with my center before pressing his erection against my core. He rocks his hips into me and my breath catches.

A soft whimper of protest escapes my lips as Dominique breaks our kiss to look down at me.

"I'll always show up." His mouth twists into a sardonic smile. "Especially when it comes with the added bonus of putting your pretty little ass in its place."

ELEVEN

DOMINIQUE

Kasey shoots me a dark look. "Careful," she warns, a hint of her bratty attitude slipping into her tone.

It's cute that she believes she holds any power here. Like her irritation is reason enough to keep me in line. Hardly.

"Or what?" Nipping at her bottom lip, I roll the skin beneath my teeth, tugging on the kiss swollen flesh before biting down hard enough to result in a hiss that slips from between her teeth but despite the sting of pain, Kasey doesn't pull away.

Baby girl, You have no idea what you've gotten yourself into.

Seeing her with Deacon this afternoon set me on edge for most of the day. Thoughts of what he was saying or doing with her before I arrived have driven me to the fringes of insanity, and I've used my time alone to consider everything I'll do to Kasey's smart little ass in payment for the suffering she's put me through.

She knows how I feel about Hunt. It's like she wanted to provoke me with that little stunt of hers. And her comment to Aaron about Deacon being *just a friend* ... bullshit. Deacon's already confirmed he's after more from her than that. Which is why I want him to stay the hell away from her.

I counted down the hours, the fucking minutes, before Aaron passed out, desperate to make my way over here and I'm going to savor every second of my time between Kasey's smooth, creamy thighs.

This is the first time I've come to her. That I've been the one with a thirst in need of quenching instead of the other way around. It should bother me. Worry me at the very least. But right now, I'm too focused on the idea of her naked body writhing beneath me to care.

These past weeks I've held myself back, keeping the monster inside me at bay.

Kasey is inexperienced. If I'd known she was a virgin at the start of things, I never would have agreed to our current arrangement. She'd been innocent. Pure. A delicate creature too fragile for my roughened hands.

I accepted the gift of her body with little protest. My control in the face of her grief is tenuous at best. The selfish bastard inside me was fueled with the need to claim the girl that I've all these years silently and recklessly considered mine.

I've never claimed the title of saint. If I had, maybe I'd have been strong enough to deny her. To deny us both. But growing up as one of Sun Valley's notorious Devils is a title and reputation I've very much earned. When a Devil wants something, he takes it. And I've ignored my own wants and needs long enough. It's time I give in to the urge to drive Kasey to the edge of madness and show her the darker sides to be found in pleasure. The ones carefully mixed with an appropriate measure of pain.

"Take your clothes off. Let me see you."

Her nostrils flare, the spark of defiance igniting in her eyes urging her to fight me on this, but tonight, I won't be relinquishing any of my control.

Kasey will accept my orders and do as she is told or mark my fucking words, there will be consequences to pay.

"It isn't a request," I growl deep in the back of my throat. "It's a fucking order. Don't make this worse on yourself by refusing me, Kasey. I am not in the mood."

Her eyes flash with fury, but there's heat in her gaze too. A full body shudder wracks her small body and a delicate blush colors her chest.

I watch for the moment she decides to comply. An intense satisfaction coursing through my veins when she offers me a barely perceptible nod.

Taking a step back, I give her enough space to sit up so she can peel back the layers of her clothes and bare her body for me. She starts by unbuttoning her pants, sliding them down her toned legs and removing one foot and then the other before gathering the hem of her shirt and tugging it over her head. She hesitates, chewing on her bottom lip while I devour her with my hungry gaze. The pink lace cups her full breasts beautifully, teasing me with the sight of her rose tipped nipples through the almost sheer material of her bra.

"Bra and panties too," I grunt, eager to have her bare.

Kasey does as she's told, surprising me as she slips the matching scrap of pink lace between her legs down and over her hips. Bending down, I retrieve her panties, tucking them into my back pocket. I realize I'm quite fond of pink and this pair of panties is mine.

Breaths coming faster now, Kasey remains quiet about my theft of her undergarments as she reaches shaking fingers to her back and unhooks the latch of her bra. Tossing it aside, she moves her arms to cover her breast but a firm shake of my head and she slowly presses her arms to her sides.

Naked and vulnerable, I allow my heated stare to wander over her again, drinking in her small and perky tits, the slight dip at her navel, and the curve of her hips. It only takes a handful of seconds before my eyes are drawn to her exquisite entrance. Kasey's bare between her thighs and if I had to bet, she's already wet and ready for me.

The electricity in the air crackles between us. The rhythm of her breaths beginning to stutter.

She swallows hard and wraps one arm around her chest while the other drops to cover her core. It looks like my scrutiny is getting to her. *There's no room for that.*

"Hands," I bark out. "At your sides."

"But—"

"Now, Kasey."

With pursed lips, she does as she's told. Her cheeks flushing. I press my knees between her thighs, kicking her legs out to widen the gap between them.

"Mmm," I made a sound of approval, staring at her pink lips already slick with her juices. It's easy to get distracted. Kasey has the most beautiful pussy. But tonight, I'll be claiming more than her cunt.

"Turn around."

She hesitates for only a second before turning around and showing me her beautiful ass. Fuck, I'm going to love seeing it red. "On the bed. All fours."

Her small hands ball into fists at her sides and she looks over her shoulder at me with an air of defiance. I see the challenge in her gaze right before she opens her mouth and says the two words sure to set my body ablaze.

"Make me."

The words have barely left her mouth before I'm on her. Grabbing a fistful of blond hair, I shove her forward onto the mattress. I'm not gentle about it either as I manhandle her into the position I want.

She fights me at first, small growls and huffs coming from her smart mouth as I work her position. With her knees on the bed and her ass facing me in the air, I give in to the urge to spank her, striking my hand on the left cheek before following it up with a quick slap to the right.

Kasey yelps and jolts forward in a vain attempt to escape me. I allow her to make it a foot closer to the edge before dragging her back again. I pull her hips back, placing that fine ass back in the air and slap her ass again, only now I strike both sides of her flesh at the same time. A minor punishment for her disobedience. I'm tempted to give her more.

As expected, her alabaster skin is contrasted by a brilliant shade of pink in the shape of my hand. *Fuck.*

"Are you going to be a good girl and take your punishment, baby girl?"

She growls low under her breath, and I can't help but chuckle.

"So defiant," I murmur, snaking one hand around her body and boldly cupping her breast. "Why is that? You know you want it." I roll her nipple between my fingers and scrape my teeth over the smooth skin of her shoulder. Once. twice. I scrape my teeth over her skin a third time before biting down and sinking my teeth into her skin. Hard.

"Fuck you," she hisses.

I release my bite and lav at the small wound with my tongue

"I'm working on it." Trailing my other hand over the curve of her ass, I inch my way to her glistening center. "Tell me how bad you want your punishment. How much you crave it."

Kasey shakes her head from side to side, her spine rigid and muscles taut. She doesn't admit that she wants it. But neither does she deny it.

Her body is wound so fucking tight. Her back arched in eager anticipation. If only she could see herself now.

"Will I find you wet for me?" I ask with a smile on my lips. "Or is your pussy weeping for me and already fucking soaked? I'm putting my money on you being soaked. Because I know you, Kasey." I pinch and twist her nipple even harder.

"You want me to take my anger out on your tight little pussy and make you come hard enough that your eyes roll in the back of your head and all you're able to see are stars."

Dipping two fingers between her folds, I thrust them deep into her cunt, filling her up. She gasps before giving in to a full body shudder, eyes wide and pupils blown.

Bracing myself with one arm, I curl over her body, enveloping her in my presence as I plunge my fingers in and out of her, finger fucking her tight little pussy at a brutal pace.

"I was right," I groan into her ear. "Fucking soaked."

Kasey responds with a deep, throaty moan. Her hips thrust backward against my crotch as I withdraw my hand from between her thighs. Yet still, she desperately chases my touch.

"But baby girl, I don't want your pussy tonight."

Her chest heaves as she looks once again over her shoulder. "Wha... what do you mean?" She can hardly catch her breath. My chest expands with satisfaction.

With her brows furrowed in confusion, I hold her stare and allow my fingers to stray from her pussy to that forbidden hole residing only a few inches up. Circling her puckered entrance, I use the juices from her pussy to slicken the way, pressing against her with the pad of my thumb.

Kasey's eyes widen. A low moan falls from her lips. I circle her entrance, again and again, keeping her on the edge of anticipation. I've taken enough of her firsts to know I won't be satisfied until I've claimed them all. "Can you handle this?" My voice is thick with desire.

With anyone else, I'd have already coated my dick with lube and slammed my cock home. But despite wanting to punish her, I need her to be onboard with this. To assure me she's strong enough to handle everything I throw her way.

Indecision is written all over her face and my impatience grows inside of me.

Watching for her reaction, I slowly sink one finger into her tight channel, giving her a taste of what I have in store.

Her lips part, but no sound comes out. I decide to take her silence as an open invitation. Thrusting one of my thick fingers into her again. I push past the tight ring of muscles that offers me resistance, pressing deeper into her ass, up to my second knuckle. Pressing against her walls, I rub her intimate flesh, stretching her out in preparation of taking me.

With my finger inside her, I feel every shift and clench of her body around me and silently will her to relax. It'll be easier if her body doesn't fight me on this.

Retreating back a few inches, I sink in again. This time plunging as deep as I can go.

Kasey whimpers and rocks her hips into my touch. Fuck. With her head turned back, our eyes are locked with one another and I sink into the depths of her baby blues, finger fucking her tight ass. I keep an eye out for any signs of discomfort or pain and there are hints of it. Between the lines of strain that bracket her mouth and the furrow between her brows, but intermixed is her obvious pleasure. Kasey's eyes are dilated and her cheeks are flushed. She accepts my intrusion with sharp gasps and breathy moans. I couldn't have asked for anything better than this.

"I'm going to fuck this ass tonight." If she's not feeling it, I need her to speak up now before I'm too far gone to let her go. Sweat dots her brow and her fingers twist in the sheets beneath her as her tits sway with the force of each thrust.

Dipping my free hand into my pocket, I retrieve a small bottle of lube I'd placed there on my way out. I'd grabbed it on an impulse, not knowing what I wanted yet for the night. And thank fuck for that foresight. Popping the cap with one hand, I withdraw my finger, pour a liberal amount of the slippery fluid between the crease of her ass, and follow it up by sinking not one but two fingers into her in a single hard thrust.

Kasey cries, the sound reverberating through the room as her walls clench around the intrusion and her body goes taut. She crumbles face first into the mattress, her arms giving out beneath her.

I don't stop. With a bruising grip on her hip, I shove both fingers in again.

Her cry is muffled by the pillow but it's still loud in the room. I want her begging for release and screaming out my name but we're in the Kappa Mu sorority house which means I'll have to settle for muffled sobs and choked off moans.

Sweeping her inner walls, I spend several minutes working my fingers in and out of her, spreading my fingers wide while buried inside her to stretch the fist like grip she has on me. If she stays this tight, she won't be able to take me. A possibility I refuse to consider. Failure is not an option.

"I'm going to fuck your ass." I wait for a response but her words are incoherent. Her mind and body are already riding an inexplicable high. Massaging the firm globes of her ass, she settles deeper against her bed, her body growing relaxed. Good.

"I'm only going to ask you once so let me know if you're paying attention."

She makes an unintelligible grunt that I assume is her way of signaling that she's listening. Stopping my thrusts but keeping my finger buried inside her I voice the words I need to say.

"Do you consent? Yes or no?"

Her breathing shutters.

"Words," I snap.

But instead of offering me her words, she arches her back impossibly further, offering her ass up toward the sky. Fuck. She has a brilliant ass. Full. Round. Enough meat to sink your fingers into. The perfect amount of cushion to slam down on your cock.

Pitching my head to the side, I take in her tight expression. Her eyes are closed, front teeth digging into her bottom lip. Sweat soaked strands of her hair cling to her face and her hands are fisted in the sheets.

"Can you take me?"

I slide my fingers out of her ass, swipe them through more of the lube, and sink them back in. This time, they slide in with little to no resistance.

"Do I have your consent?" I growl, desperate to line her up with the head of my cock and bury myself inside.

Kasey sucks in a lungful of air exhaling it through her teeth. A low moan works its way up her throat followed by a single word laced in desperate anticipation.

"Yes."

Thank fuck.

Withdrawing my fingers entirely, I make quick work of removing my clothes. Discarding them beside the bed, I pop the cap on the lubricant again and coat my already hard cock in a thick layer.

Kasey tilts her head to watch me, eyes wide and tinged with fear.

"Say what's on your mind."

She hesitates, chest heaving and indecision flickering in her gaze.

"Will it fit?" she asks. In the position she's in, she can't see my raging hard on which is probably for the best. No need to freak her out more.

With a dark chuckle, I rub the head of my cock up and down her folds.

"Oh, baby girl. We'll make it fit."

Grabbing a fistful of her hair, I jerk her toward me until our bodies are almost flush. "The only question is," My words are like gravel against her ear, "how long will it take before you cry out for mercy."

Keeping one hand in her hair, I reach the other around her body until my fingers find the swollen nub of her clit. There's going to be pain once I take her. No way to get around it. Losing your anal virginity isn't any easier than having your cherry popped. There's discomfort. Usually a little pain.

I don't have experience taking it in the ass nor do I ever plan to. No judgment on dudes who take it but it's not a direction I swing.

But I've buried my dick in enough women's asses to know being taken like this is a lesson in brutal intimacy. And fuck can it be good.

I'll make it good for Kasey too. Show her what it's like to ride that line between pleasure and pain when you're pushed to that inexplicable ledge where you believe it's too much, that there's no way you can possibly take any more, only to shatter into a million pieces as wave after wave of sensation and pleasure electrifies the very marrow in your bones.

By the time the head of my cock parts her ass, she'll have already cum twice, making her boneless, her body wrung out and unable to fight my intrusion.

Strumming her clit, I settle on into a steady rhythm that has Kasey writhing against me. Throwing her head against my shoulder, she arches her back, pushes out her breasts as her lips part and she releases a guttural moan.

Breathing heavy, she chases her release. Her movements grow more erratic with every second that passes and her moans of pleasure ratchet up in volume.

Without the pillow in her face, we're liable to get caught. Releasing my hold on her hair, I cover her mouth, digging my fingers into the soft tissue of her cheeks as I stifle her cries.

Kasey's hot breath coats my palm and there's something about the sound of her muffled moans against my hand that makes my cock impossibly harder.

I know the exact moment her orgasm slams into her. Her blunt fingernails dig crescent moons into my forearm and her back bows, neck muscles straining as she releases a scream into my hand.

I can't wait to fuck her.

Screw it.

Flipping her onto her back before she's had the chance to come down from her release, I plunge my cock into her cunt, filling her up. Her pussy convulses around me, aftershocks of her orgasm continuing to rocket through her as I pound mercilessly into her again and again. I pick up a furious pace, gritting my teeth as I stave off my own release, determined to feel the walls of her pussy flutter around my cock when I make her cum again.

"Oh, god. Dom—" I cut off her pleasure soaked plea with my hand clamped over her mouth before bringing my face so close to hers that I can make out the multitude of blues that make up the iris of her eyes.

Without bothering to slow down my thrusts, I hold her tear filled gaze and snap, "Do you want everyone in this house to know how desperate you are for my cock?"

Eyes wide, she tries to shake her head, but my grip on her face gives her little room to move.

Good enough.

"Then I suggest you keep your mouth shut and stop screaming before you announce to the whole fucking house exactly what it is that we're doing."

Blinking up at me like she understands, I keep up my pace, thrusting into her tight heat as she clenches around me, fisting my cock in her warm embrace.

Her nails dig into my skin and I welcome the small sting of pain. Leaning forward, I replace my hand with my mouth, devouring Kasey's strangled moans with my kiss. She thrashes wildly beneath me, her teeth clashing against my own.

Hooking one of her legs over my hip, I adjust the angle of my thrusts. A groan vibrates in my chest as Kasey claws at my back. I'm hitting that sweet spot of hers that can only be reached at this particular angle. It only takes a few more pumps of my cock before she throws her head back in abandon, veins straining against her neck.

"Come for me, baby girl."

"I can't," she gasps, tossing her head from side to side in a clear display of desperation.

Yeah. That isn't going to work for me.

"Yes, you can," I growl.

Pulling back until only the tip of my cock remains inside her, I plunge myself deep into her depths, closing my eyes. Her cunt sucks me impossibly deeper, welcoming me into her warm and wet embrace.

Kasey's eyes roll into the back of her head, her body shuddering. I repeat the motions again and again. Pounding into her pussy harder than I've ever dared to before.

It's as though I'm exorcizing my demons, releasing them through the connection between our bodies and I fail to remember where she begins and where I end.

Fuck, the way this girl messes with my head.

Wrapping my fingers around her neck, I squeeze hard enough to cut off her air supply. "You're going to come again. And when you do," I pause just long enough for her to lift her tear stained eyes up to my gaze.

God she's a fucking mess.

Mascara is smudged beneath her eyes and tear tracks run down either side of her face. Her skin is flushed an unflattering shade of red. Her lips are bruised and swollen.

And she's never been more beautiful to me than she is at this moment.

"I'm going to finish what I started and take this tight little ass," I squeeze one round cheek in my hand, hard enough that Kasey flinches but her cunt flutters around me, the beginning signs of her impending release.

Relaxing my grip, I knead her skin, rocking my hips into her body while her thigh muscles relax, spreading herself wide for me. Her lashes flutter and I flex my fingers on her throat enough to allow a quick gasp of air before squeezing tight once again.

"That's it, baby girl. Take what you need. Come on my dick so I can bury myself in that beautiful ass."

My vulgar words have their desired effect.

Her pussy seizes around me, thighs jerking together to clamp around my hips as her release rolls through her like a blazing wildfire scorching everything in its path.

Her body squeezes me like a fist, causing my vision to go black while I fight back the waves of my own release. *Not yet.* Hissing through my teeth, I dig into my control, determined to get what I came for tonight. My fingers are still wrapped around the column of her throat and slowly release them, one finger at a time. Satisfaction thrums through me as her eyes lose focus and her lips part on a gasp before her chest swells, sucking in a desperate lungful of air.

"Look at you." Her pussy makes a suctioning sound as I pull myself free from her folds. Evidence of her release clings to my dick and all but drips down my length.

Her body spent and exhausted, I roll Kasey onto her side before moving to lie beside her. Taking position at her back. I position her hips against my own, cradling her ass against my crotch while I pull her riot of curls behind her back and away from her face.

"You loved that didn't you? My dirty little slut. You liked that I was rough with you."

She makes a sound of agreement in the back of her throat, her heavy lids fluttering as sleep threatens to pull her under.

No rest for the wicked, baby girl.

Unconcerned, I retrieve the lubricant from where I dropped it earlier and coat my two fingers in the thick substance.

Lifting one of her thighs, I hook it over my hip, bending my own knee at an angle and spreading her wide.

"Now comes the part of the night where I deliver your punishment."

Fingers trailing along her crease, I glide my hand up and down, mixing the lube with the remnant of her release.

"Are you going to be a good girl and take it?"

Her voice is a throaty whisper when she says, "I'll be good."

The corners of my mouth curl into a smile. "Good. Bite that bottom lip of yours and stay quiet."

Seeing her do as I command, I shift my attention to ensuring Kasey is slick and ready for me. Briefly fingering her ass, I once again stretch out her tight channel.

I don't know how I'll stuff my cock in here, but one way or another, I'm determined to make it work.

Kasey moans at the first intrusion, her body limp and sated against me as I start with one finger and then work my way up to two.

She clenches beautifully around my fingers, fighting the intrusion before I remind her to relax.

"That's it. Look at you. Good girl." I scrape my teeth over her shoulder, sucking at the earlier mark I left. She shivers against me, goosebumps breaking out of her sweat-soaked skin.

Spreading my fingers inside her, my lips ghost over the shell of her ear. "Look at that ass suck in my fingers. You like that, don't you, baby girl? Does that feel good? Do you like it when I play in your tight little hole?"

"Mmm mmm," she mumbles incoherently, but I know she's getting into it. Her chest rises and falls at a rapid clip as her body begins to follow the motions of my hand, clenching around every thrust of my fingers and chasing after my touch with every retreat.

She's almost where I need her to be. Drunk on lust while languid in my arms. Her body moves on pure instinct, her mind unable to form coherent thoughts. Kasey's eyes are glazed over.

Just a little more.

The wait is excruciating. My rock hard erection presses against the seam of her ass, eager for entry. Precum leaks from my tip, leaving a wet trail over the curve of her ass.

When she's as relaxed as she can be, I withdraw my fingers and apply a liberal amount of lube to my aching cock. Spreading her cheeks, I coat her entrance and move myself into position, lining up my erection with her puckered hole.

Pressing forward, the mushroom head of my cock slips past the tight ring of muscle. A groan builds in my throat and Kasey sucks in a sharp breath.

"That's it," I coo as I sink another inch into her. "Look at how good you take me. You were made for my cock, baby girl. Relax. Surrender your body to me. Let me in."

She whimpers, her breaths loud and erratic.

Fuck.

Sucking in a ragged breath, I force myself to slow down long enough for her to relax around me. Kissing her back, her shoulder, her neck, I hold myself still until her breaths even. Flexing my fingers on the inside of her thigh, I sink another inch deeper.

Her hands fist the sheets beneath her and, peering over her shoulder, I find her eyes squeezed shut, a furrow of pain sitting between her brows.

That's not going to work.

"How are you feeling, baby girl?"

"F—full." Tremors wrack her delicate body and an idea forms in my head.

"Oh yeah?"

She nods.

"Look at me, baby girl."

Doing as she's told, Kasey twists her neck and peers up at me through a thick veil of lashes.

I'm a firm believer that obedience should be rewarded. Rocking my hips against her, I sink my cock the rest of the way inside of her, gritting my teeth and refusing to stop until I've buried myself to the hilt, skin on skin and not so much as an inch separating our bodies.

Kasey exhales a strangled breath, a whimper lodging itself in her throat..

Giving her a moment to adjust, I trail my fingers along the sensitive skin of her thighs, enjoying the stark contrast of my rich, dark skin against her soft, pale complexion.

"How about we make you fuller?"

With my free hand, I cup her breast, tweaking her nipple until she gasps and moans against me.

"I'm going to fuck you now," I groan into her hair. "And if you're a good little slut and take what I give you, I'll consider letting you come for a third time tonight. Would you like that?"

TWELVE
KASEY

I'm going to die. It's the only explanation I have for what I'm experiencing right now. I've somehow died and gone to heaven. Or maybe it's hell. I honestly don't know anymore.

My body is spent. Muscles and limbs too tired to do anything more than lie here as Dominique withdraws his hips, sliding his erection out of my forbidden entrance until nothing but the tip of his cock remains. He hovers there for a beat, allowing anticipation to build inside me before he sinks himself back in, igniting my body and electrifying my nerve endings with a single thrust.

I cry out, but whether from pain or pleasure, I don't know. Up feels like down and down feels like up. My body is alight with sensation. My mind is drunk with lust, desperation, and need.

There is this growing feeling in the bottom of my belly that demands one thing and one thing only. *More.* I've never experienced anything like this before.

Dominique lets go of my breast to get a firmer grip on my thigh, squeezing my flesh and keeping me spread open as he fucks me with slow, powerful strokes.

His other hand slides beneath my head and for a second, I think he's going to stretch it out beneath the pillow, but instead, his hand curls to wrap around my throat, pressing beneath my chin and forcing my gaze further up until I'm twisted at an awkward angle, our gazes now able to touch.

He doesn't squeeze. Not at first. But the threat lingers, hanging in the air. A reminder that he can cut off my air supply anytime he wants. My pussy clenches. A shot of adrenaline racing down my spine. Something about his hold, the pure possessiveness of it, has a warm rush of heat dripping down the insides of my thighs.

Oh, my god. He's right. I might actually come for a third time tonight. How is that even possible? But I feel a familiar pressure building low in my belly. It's different from before. Deeper. Darker. A sensation filled with promise if only I surrender to it.

It's as if my body wants me to endure the storm rather than run after it.

Dominique pants beside me, his heated breath brushing along my bare skin.

His dark brown eyes are hooded and his powerful body flexes and strains with each thrust of his powerful hips. A muscle ticks in his jaw and if I could reach him, I'd trail my finger along the nerve, tracing the evidence of his response to being inside of me.

"I'm going to fill your tight hole with my cum," he growls into my ear. "Going to fill you up."

My body goes white hot at the thought and my thighs squeeze as if he's already cum and I'm desperate to hold in his release.

Bearing his teeth, Dominique snarls against my skin, picking up his pace.

A sharp spear of pain shoots from my ass to my pussy before blazing a tingling path down to the tips of my toes.

An uncomfortable ache ignites my nerve endings. It's not painful per say. But the burn in my ass ripples through me the way a skipped rock ripples across the surface of a pond, creating a disturbance that affects everything surrounding the point of origin.

The ripples that move through my body now leave a smattering of little fires that burn within my veins.

"You like the sound of that, don't you, baby girl?"

I'm almost disgusted to admit, I do. I really freaking do. I love the sound of his voice when he growls filthy words at me. I love it when he's rough and aggressive with my body. And I can't deny the thrill that tingles down my spine every time he makes a demand or orders me to undress for him. To bare my intimate flesh to his hungry gaze.

I never thought I'd see the day where I gave in to Dominique Price, but if I thought the sex before was amazing, what he's doing to me tonight is a religious experience.

The problem is, I'm drowning in a storm of emotions I've never felt before. Swimming in the deep end and sinking into the deep blue sea, too far to have any chance of swimming up to break the surface and sucking in a desperate breath of fresh air.

I am overwhelmed by the need for Dominic to fill me with his cum. I am desperate for him to lay claim to every inch of my body. To mark me with his hands, abuse me with his teeth and devour me with his kiss.

There is something seriously wrong with what is happening inside of me right now.

Possessed. Owned. Controlled.

I want to feel all of those things and I want to feel them with him. It's a terrifying thought.

Passion unfurls deep inside my chest, spreading roots of delicious desire throughout my limbs. What the hell is happening to me?

My lips move fast as I whisper his name in a mindless chant full of abandon.

Dominique. Dominique. Dominique. Yes. Please. Dominique. I never want it to end. Emotion clouds my mind and my brain kicks into overdrive eager to define this strange feeling that thrashes within me, a relentless inferno capable of laying waste to my mind, body, and soul.

It's not love. I could never love Dominique Price. But whatever it is, it's a cloying addiction. Deceptively sweet as it sinks its claws into me, offering me a taste I will never be able to get enough of.

I can't. We have to—

Dominique grabs my hands and guides it between my thighs, pressing my fingers into my drenched pussy. I moan when I accidentally press on my clit and Dominique grunts a sound of approval.

"Play with that pussy for me," he demands. "I want to feel your ass milking my cock when you make yourself cum."

My clit is so sensitive, the very idea of touching myself makes a tremor roll down my spine. There's no way I can do it.

When Dominique sees me hesitate, he growls in frustration and brushes my hand aside. I only have a moment of relief before the sharp sound of skin on skin assaults my ears.

Smack.

I yelp, jerking away from the pain, but there's nowhere to go with him pressed to my back. Before I say anything, let alone demand any sort of explanation, Dominique pulls his hand back and slaps me again, striking my pussy and abusing my clit all in the same move..

"Dominique!" I try to close my legs, but he grabs hold of my thigh, splaying me wide again. The fingers around my throat tighten in warning and his hips come to a stop with him buried to the hilt inside me.

"Is there a reason you're refusing to do as you're told?" His voice is sharp and threaded with a warning that I am in too much discomfort to heed.

"I'm too sensitive," I whine. Squirming in his hold, I struggle to create distance between us, but I'm not getting away until Dominique allows me too.

"Too fucking bad."

I assume that's the end. I've disappointed him. Big deal. But instead of moving on or continuing to fuck me, Dominique brings his hand back between my thighs.

I flinch, bracing for another slap, but instead he plunges two fingers into my soaked cunt and thrusts them in and out of me, eliciting a gasp followed quickly by a moan. Oh, my god.

I writhe beneath him.

"Looks like I'll have to do the work myself."

He finger fucks me with punishing strokes all while still rocking his hips in shallow strokes against my ass. All at once I'm in sensory overload. My nerves are on fire at the same time that ice floods my veins. I'm hot and then cold. Fighting between the urge to chase my own pleasure and resisting the slow burn of pain.

It's too much.

Opening my mouth, I struggle to force out the words to tell him I can't take anymore but I manage a, "Too much—" before the fingers of his other hand tighten around my neck tight enough to cut off my breath, and long enough that dark spots dance across my vision.

"No, baby girl. It's just enough."

His next thrust against my ass is savage, and at the same time, he works his finger into my pussy and presses his thumb down on my clit. Those three actions at once send me into a free fall. Stars explode behind my eyes and my orgasm slams into me like a violent storm.

A sob tries to tear itself from my throat, but without any air in which to release it, it comes out as little more than a strangled hiss of breath.

My head is light. Fuzzy. Without oxygen, I can't make a sound, but my lips still form the shape of his name, silently chanting it again and again as white-hot pleasure blazes through me.

Dominique. Dominique. Dominique.

Just when I think I'm going to pass out, he releases his hold on my throat, withdraws his fingers from my pussy, and grabs my hip, sinking his cock in as far as it'll go. He shoves me forward onto my stomach, and sinks himself deep inside of me three more times before stiffening on top of me.

With a deep groan, his cock jerks inside of me, spurting his release and filling me with his cum like he said he would before slumping onto the bed, his body still half on top of me.

Dom doesn't pull himself free. Instead, he tugs me back onto my side until our bodies are flush. One arm wraps around my middle and he presses his face to my hair.

I look down at the contrast of our skin, his dark arm against my pale skin and Deacon's words slither into the recesses of my mind.

Dominique will never settle down with a white woman.

Exhaustion pulls at me and for once, I listen to its call, sinking into the promise of sleep and ignoring what will come tomorrow.

THIRTEEN
DOMINIQUE

I don't mean to fall asleep.

When I pull Kasey toward me, my plan is to take a couple of minutes, catch my breath, and then slip free from her body and return to my own bed for the night.

That isn't what happens. I don't know how much time I lose, but when I next open my eyes, it's to the sight of Kasey's blond curls tangled beneath my chin.

Her naked body presses against mine, a warm weight I'm loath to admit I enjoy feeling beside me. She's burrowed herself into the crook of my arm with her head resting on top of my chest. One creamy thigh drapes elegantly between mine, tucking the tips of her toes beneath my calf. This is full-blown cuddling if I've ever seen it.

Fuck.

We must have shifted in our sleep. The way Kasey looks now, eyes closed and delicate lips parted, you'd think she wants me to hold her. That she enjoys being wrapped up in arms. Maybe she even takes comfort in the steady thrum of my heart beneath her ear.

She must have grown cold in the middle of the night. Why else would she seek out my warmth? We've slept in the same bed before, and sure there's been some spooning, but usually, I hold her captive against me and when I wake up, she's on her side of the bed and I'm on mine. Never before has she curled into me like this.

I don't know how to feel about it. My thumb traces the dark mark on her shoulder. It's a medley of purple and yellow. A mark I left when I sank my teeth into her skin.

My mind races with memories of last night. The way I dug my hands into her hips and squeezed her throat, denying her breath. Her pussy was drenched for me, and she took my cock in her ass perfectly. I knew that she would.

But fuck. What I did...I can't believe I took her so brutally like that, but not a single part of me regrets it. Baby Henderson took everything I dished out and would have willingly taken more.

Where did she come from? And how the hell was I lucky enough to be the first to claim her? That thought leaves a bitter taste in my mouth. A possessive need to not only be her first but also her last and everything else in between surges through my veins. *Snap out of it.*

I'm not playing for keeps here. This is a temporary game.

Sunlight filters through the room letting me know that night has long since come and gone.

Moving slowly, I slide Kasey's head from my chest and onto her pillow. She shifts to get comfortable, a small furrow forming between her brows. Holding my breath, I remain still, waiting to see if she'll wake. When she settles, I exhale a breath of relief and slip the rest of the way out from beneath her. Stifling my groan when my dick sticks to her thigh, I force myself out of her bed, ignoring my morning wood as my eyes hunt for my clothes.

What time is it? A look at her bedside clock shows it's 5:14 a.m.. *Shit.* Later than I thought. Or earlier, depending on how you want to look at it.

On an upside, Kappa Mu is on the edge of campus, so it won't take me long to get to the field. But it also means I won't have time to shower until after practice. I'm not bothered by that realization as much as I should be. I like the smell of her on my skin. The lingering scent of her strawberry shampoo. The erotic fragrance of her pussy. I didn't get the chance to bury my face between her thighs. But I'll make sure to indulge in eating her pretty little cunt the next time I have her spread out beneath me.

Throwing on my shirt and black athletic shorts from last night, I give Kasey one last lingering look. My dick decides now is the perfect time to bob beneath my shorts, directing his attention to the women spread out beside us.

I adjust myself, but it only seems to make it worse, taking my dick from a semi to a full blown erection. You would think after the marathon of sex last night, my dick would be a gentleman and take a break, but all it wants is another round in the sack with Kasey. Maybe two.

Sucking on my teeth, I consider what I'm supposed to do. We haven't done this at her place before. Me sleeping over. Usually she's in my bed and I just get up and leave for practice without waking her. But this is her space. Will it piss her off to wake up and see that I'm gone? Do I leave a note? Should I wake her up?

Nah. Bad idea. I should let her sleep.

Right?

Right.

Nodding to myself, I abandon both ideas and move for the door. This is the right call. Post sex conversations are awkward. Kasey knows I have practice in the mornings. It's why I'm gone first thing in the morning when she crashes at my place.

She won't be surprised to wake up and see that I'm gone, and she sure as shit won't be disappointed. Most likely, she'll be relieved.

Brows drawn, I waste several seconds that I don't have trying to parse out whether that bothers me.

Nah. I'm good. It could be nice if she gave a shit about where I'd gone. But there's no reason for her to keep tabs on me.

Dragging my hand over my face, I stifle a groan. What am I still doing here?

Decision made, I slip through her door, closing it behind me.

Voices reach my ears, coming from deeper inside of the house. Taking that as my cue to haul ass and leave. I make a beeline for the side exit door.

Outside, I tug my hood low over my head and scan the yard for anyone who's decided today is the day to enjoy the great outdoors, but from the look of things, I'm all clear. Careful to keep my face tipped down to the ground in case anyone comes outside and sees me, I jog across the small concrete patio toward my Escalade. Turning the ignition, I back out of the parking space and head for Suncrest U's football stadium.

If I'm lucky, Coach will be too busy with the rest of the team to ream my ass about being late to practice. If I'm unlucky, I'll be running a shit load of laps.

I hate fucking laps.

SWEAT POURS down my face as I circle the field for the sixteenth time, marking my fourth mile. Coach barely even looked my way when I arrived. Just pointed at the track and told me to get moving. Roman and Emilio are enjoying the shit out of this. Both those fuckers have pointed and laughed in my direction more than a few times already.

Hunt is standing in as QB while I run, and I've got to give it to the kid, he's come a long way this season. I still think he's an asshole, and I sure as shit don't want him anywhere near Kasey, but he's getting better. If he pulls his head out of his ass, he'll be a great starting quarterback next season after I graduate.

"Price!" Coach shouts my name.

I veer off my path and sprint across the field, coming to a stop in front of him.

"How's the shoulder?" he asks.

Using the hem of my shirt to wipe the sweat from my face, I tell him the truth. Mostly. "Better. Tight when I overdo it, but the pain is minor and Doc gave me the all clear to throw."

He grunts. Not sure if it's a happy grunt or an angry one. You never know with him. "We've got PacNorth coming up."

I nod, as if we didn't just have this conversation the other day. "You're playing the first half, but if that shoulder gives you any trouble, I want you to call it and Hunt can finish out the last two quarters. Am I clear?"

"Got it."

"Good. Now get your ass on the field and warm up with your receivers."

Giving him a salute, I grab a ball and jog to the center of the field. Today the team has been running drills, saving the practice plays for later on. Catching Roman's gaze, he gives me the all ready and races down the field. Ignoring what else is happening around me, I pull back and shoot the ball through the air, the laces spinning in a perfect spiral.

A sharp zing arrows into the point where my shoulder connects with my chest and I roll my arm to chase the ache away.

Roman tracks the ball, head lifted to the sky as he races toward the end zone. Jumping in the air, he makes the catch at the ten yard line. His momentum throws him and he tucks into a backward roll before springing to his feet. Holding the ball, he lets out a triumphant cheer and tosses it to the sidelines before jogging back, readying himself for me to throw again.

"Now it's your turn to run," I jest.

"Hey. I wasn't the one who showed up late." Even through the guard on his helmet, I can see his smirk. "Where were you, by the way?"

I retrieve another ball from the bag Coach keeps on the field, buying myself time before I answer. "Overslept. Guess I didn't hear my alarm go off."

He tilts his head to the side, not quite believing me. I'm a light sleeper. Roman knows that. But I don't give him time to question me. "Go wide," I call out, arcing the ball across the field and shooting it long and to my far left.

Like a bolt of lightning, Roman takes off. His fingers kiss the leather and for a second I think he'll fumble, but he dives forward, saving the catch as his chest collides with the turf.

"Hell yeah!" he shouts, hyping himself up, and I have to give it to him. That one was impressive.

The rest of practice goes much the same way. Me throwing uncatchable throws and Roman landing them anyway. Half way through, three of our other receivers join the mix, tapping Roman out so he can take a slight break before going to catch for Hunt.

I don't have as good of a system in place with the other guys as I do with Roman. I've played with Wilmos and Bedford since sophomore year, but Caulder is a recent addition this year like Hunt and we haven't found our groove yet. The guy never seems to know what my signals mean, nor can he anticipate my throws, which makes him useless to me on the field.

Thirty minutes later, Coach calls time and sends us all to the locker room. Last night's sweat and fluids cling to my skin beneath today's fresh layer of grime. I go straight for the showers, eager to wash it all away. Like silent wraiths, Roman and Emilio follow me.

Sensing the impending interrogation, I try to head them off. "How's the baby?" I ask E, turning the water on and stepping under the spray.

"Perfect," he says, following suit. "But fuck, the little devil never sleeps."

Roman and I chuckle. "Ain't no rest for the wicked."

"Then how the hell did you get so much shut eye and still wind up late this morning?" he asks.

I walked right into that one.

Soaping up my body, I take longer than I should to come up with a generic answer. "Slept in," I grunt. They should believe that. Hell, they both overslept at least twice a month when we were back in high school.

Roman elbows Emilio in the ribs before dipping his chin toward me. "This cabrón says he slept through his alarm," he tells him. "*Methiroso.*"

"What the hell does that mean?"

Emilio frowns. "Yeah. You're right."

My eyes ping-pong back and forth between them. Fucking Spanish speaking fuckers. I haven't heard that word before. There should be rules for this shit. No secret language conversations in front of your friends. It's rude. I only know the usual slang. *Cabrón. Pendejo. Estúpido.* You know, the bad words in Spanish you want to learn.

Roman chuckles at the dark look on my face. "We're calling you a liar," he deadpans.

"Yeah, man. Liar, liar. Pants on fire." Emilio smirks.

"I'm not lying." I grind the words between my teeth. I slept in. It wasn't intentional, but that doesn't make it any less true.

"Testy," Emilio chides. "You need to go back to bed? A good nap always helps Luis turn his frown upside down."

I give him a withering stare. Does it phase him? Not in the least. The man's got two kids now and lives in a house with both of his older brothers. Not much save for his woman can penetrate his carefree exterior. I settle for flipping him off. It makes me feel better at least.

"Alright. Alright. Perfect Price slept in for once." Emilio holds both hands in the air, palms turned to face me. "My bad. Don't get your panties in a twist about it."

"I did."

"Sure. We believe you." His words say one thing, but the grin on his face says another.

"Whatever."

With a smirk, he looks to Roman and some sort of silent communication passes between them. Clenching my teeth, I ignore them. I'm usually in on whatever silent shit is being passed along, so whatever they're relaying, it isn't for me. Or more accurately, it's about me, which is why I'm not supposed to know.

Assholes.

"So ..." Emilio says, and I can tell by the tone of his voice that he wants to ask me a question. "Who you taking to the fundraiser?"

"What fundraiser?" I ask.

Roman rocks back on his heels and whistles. That *oh shit* whistle that lets you know you've gone and fucked up.

"Bro. The McIntire Dinner. Please tell me you did not forget. Your ass, along with the rest of the team's, is required to be there."

Shit. I forgot. "It's fine. When is it?"

"The Monday after our game."

Cursing, I count how much time I have between then and now. Then I remember that fucking meeting with Andres DeAnde. So much for having time this weekend to figure anything out. I have a few suits hanging in my closet, so I'm good on clothes, but I'll need a date. The one and only time I've gone to one of these events solo, I learned right away never to make that mistake again.

The cougars at these kinds of things are vicious and will do anything they can to sink their claws into a young, fresh piece of meat. Hard pass. I'm not looking to be anyone's future meal ticket, nor do I need a sugar momma.

"You got a date?" Roman asks.

I nod. He knows as well as I do that a date to these things is required. Lucky bastard has Allie to bring though, so he doesn't have to worry about tracking down a plus one. Same goes for Emilio. He has Bibiana, though she just had baby Roberto—named after Emilio's oldest brother—so she might not be ready to leave the baby yet for the couple of hours the dinner will take.

"I'll get it covered." Toweling off, I retrieve my phone from my locker and type out a quick text.

Me: McIntire dinner Monday night. You game?

SHE RESPONDS RIGHT AWAY.

Tamara: Already on my calendar. Figured you'd get around to asking me.

Me: Thanks T. You're a lifesaver.

Tamara: Don't I know it. Your parents going to be there?

I STARE AT HER QUESTION, irritated to have forgotten that fun fact. They didn't used to go, but my parents have made it a point to attend all of the team's required events. I rarely show up to their weekly dinners, and this is their way of still cornering me to get an update and whatever other information they want to know about my life.

Me: Probably.

Tamara: Cool. Semi-modest dress it is.

WITH A SIGH, I toss my phone in my bag and tug on a fresh set of clothes before closing my locker. Turning around, my eyes land on Roman and Emilio. Both are dressed now but giving me expectant looks like they're waiting for something, but I'll be damned if I know what it is.

"What?" I brush past them, forcing the pair to keep pace if they have anything else to say.

"Who are you taking?" Emilio asks.

My brows furrow. "Same chick I always take."

Lines bracket his mouth and his lips tug down at the corners into a frown. Emilio rubs the back of his neck. A nervous gesture of his, but it's Roman who asks, "You're not taking baby Henderson?"

Coming to a hard stop, I spin on my heel and turn to face my best friends. I need to lock this shit down right here. Right now.

"What the hell would make you think I wanted to spend my Monday night trapped at a fundraiser with Baby fucking Henderson?" I snap.

Roman's eyes flash at my tone. "You've been spending a lot of time with her."

"And you've always had a thing for the girl," Emilio adds.

"I did not have a thing for her."

E rolls his eyes. "Bro, we all went to the same school. Anytime Kasey walked into a room, your eyes were glued to her fucking ass."

"Your point?" My upper lip quivers into a snarl. "She's Aaron's fucking sister. And I'm not the only one who's checked out her ass." I give both guys knowing looks.

"Neither one of us has ever wanted to fuck her."

"Thinking and doing are two different things," I remind him. "I checked out her ass a few times in high school. None of that explains why you'd expect her to be my date. You know I've taken Tamara to every athletic function Coach has made us go to since freshman year."

"Yeah, but you don't want to fuck her."

Irrelevant. Tamara doesn't want to fuck me either. We have a mutually beneficial arrangement. She pretends to be my fake girlfriend at the events and whenever she needs it, I pose for the occasional picture and she passes me off to her family as her long-term boyfriend. We've been dating for three years, but have no immediate plans to get engaged because we're responsible young adults and want to graduate college before embarking on our lives together. We're career driven the way both our parents expect us to be and so far, no one has questioned the decisions we present.

Tamara has her master's degree after she gets her bachelors, and I'll most likely drag my education out and get my MBA. Whatever it takes to postpone the inevitable.

Either way, we have time to drag this relationship out until we break the news to our families that things between us just didn't work out.

Her parents live in Canada, so pictures and the occasional video call are all I've needed to endure. If you ask me, I'm getting the better deal out of this. She shows up to four or five events with me throughout the year and at almost every one of them, she's forced to play the role of girlfriend. The hand holding. The fake smiles. The occasional kiss. Tamara gets to play at the whole nine yards.

I never planned to make her my fake girlfriend. I only wanted her to stand in as my plus one to athletic events. We met in class and wound up partnering up for labs and realized we got along. A pleasant surprise since I have a hard time tolerating new people. And rarely pass the stage of tolerance and move into liking them. There's a reason I have three friends in my life. Roman, Emilio, and Aaron. If you count

Alejandra and Bibi, I have two more and zero need to add to the list. But T is laid back. Chill.

She was the one who suggested our current arrangement. And it was what we both needed at the time. Still is.

Tamara comes from a conservative family. One who won't support her actual relationship with Holly Webster, her girlfriend. I'm her hetero stand in at least until she graduates from college. After that, if her parents disown her, she'll have graduated already and be fine. She already has to foot her own masters degree, so her only goal is to get through this year and the next before she comes out and lets the chips fall where they may.

She wanted a fake relationship. I only needed a stand-in. But then Richard and Sheridan Price came to an annual fundraiser and decided Tamara Vinzent is the kind of woman you settle down with. It was easier to go along with the lie with the added bonus of getting my parents off my back than it was to untangle myself with the truth and risk jeopardizing Tamara's side of our imaginary relationship.

Mom's tried setting me up on dates with daughters of her friends from the country club and I've wasted a significant amount of my time getting out of them.

All of that stopped once I introduced T as my girlfriend. *Problem, meet your solution.* Everything else is history. The guys know the situation, though. They shouldn't act surprised she's my date, and no way should they believe I'd consider taking Kasey.

Required attendance or not, asking Kasey would make it a date. A very public, very real, date. I'm no idiot. And a date with Kasey Henderson is never going to happen.

FOURTEEN
KASEY

It's early, the sun is too bright and cheery for my liking, and everything *hurts*.

And when I say everything, I mean *everything*.

My back is on fire. My voice cracks when I talk because my throat is still raw from screaming last night. I can hardly feel my leg muscles as I walk to class. They're like jelly. I keep waiting to fall on my face.

And that wonderful place between my thighs. Yeah, she's not feeling so wonderful right now. And don't even get me started on my ass. Oh. My. God. My cheeks heat just thinking about what I let Dominique do to me, and the traitorous hussy living between my thighs clenches like she's ready to do it all again.

I was exhausted after last night's events and slept through my alarm. By the time I woke up, I had less than twenty minutes to get to class.

I took the fastest shower of my life, got dressed, and ran across campus to get to my first class on time. My professor was not impressed, but I made it, and after my first class ended, he called me aside and gave me a get caught up plan. I have an insane amount of homework and reading to catch up on, but it looks like all of my teachers are willing to offer make-up assignments and extra credit opportunities.

I should be relieved. My professor took care of all the arrangements. I don't have to go through the motions of explaining my circumstances to my other teachers and, most importantly, to Mr. Fisks. Who I already knew didn't like me and probably likes me even less after Deacon carted me out of his class the other day.

This way, I already have all the assignments and just need to email them to the appropriate professor as I complete them. As long as I get everything in by the end of the semester, I'll be fine.

Twisting my still wet hair into a messy bun, I head for Fisks' classroom. Deacon's already here and, like before, I drop into the vacant seat beside him.

"You look..." He takes in my wet hair, bare face, and oversized sweater. I'm wearing shorts too, but the hoodie is so big on me you can't tell. Not my best look. Nor are the mismatched shoes, but I was in such a rush this morning that I didn't realize I'd grabbed two different colored converse sneakers. One red and one black. At least they're the same brand. "Better."

I crack a full-faced smile. "Thanks." And pretend he didn't finish that statement in his head with a different word.

Better. Ha. I look like one of the late night Walmart shoppers people like to take pictures of when nobody is looking so they can make memes about them before blasting them all over the internet, but sure, we'll go with better.

"What'd you do last night?" he asks.

Trust me. You do not want to know. Out loud, I tell him, "Just hung out in my room catching up on homework."

He nods. "Did you get it all sorted out?"

"Yep." Leaning down, I grab the notebook I use for this class and dig around the bottom of my bag for a pen.

"Do anything else besides homework?"

Finding one, I sit back up and toss it on my desktop, ignoring the dull ache in my lower back from leaning over. "Nope."

Deacon makes a weird sound in the back of his throat.

"You okay there?" I ask.

Lines bracket his mouth and I catch the flash of annoyance on his face before he turns away from me, directing his gaze to the front of the class. "I'm fine." His words are clipped, ice all but dripping from his chilly tone.

"What just happened?"

A tick forms in his jaw. He doesn't look at me as he says, "Nothing. Thought we agreed to be friends, but you cleared that up for me."

I did what? "I have no idea what you're talking about." I didn't. One second things are fine and the next Jack Frost over here is making an appearance and giving me the cold shoulder.

"You lied to me."

My mouth drops open. "When?"

"Just now."

I mean, yeah. Sorta. But it's not like I was malicious about it. "Okay. I lied." But he's blowing things out of proportion here. "Do you want to know what time I ate dinner or how many times I went to the bathroom?" Am I supposed to give you a play-by-play for every hour of my day? Geez.

He turns in his seat and his honey-colored eyes level me with a look I've never seen from him before. He's angry. No. Angry doesn't cover it. He looks *pissed*.

"No. But it would've lessened the blow if you'd been honest with me."

"About what?" Why is he being so dumb about this?

"About getting together with the asshole I'd just told you was my brother. You swore you wouldn't say anything to him and then you go and do me like that. I thought we were cool, Kasey. That you were different."

His angry words hover between us and I'm so stunned by his expression and the complete and utter look of betrayal on his face that it takes my mind a few extra seconds to realize he's not mad I slept with Dominique and didn't tell him. He thinks I spilled his secrets.

I open my mouth to explain. To assure him, I didn't tell Dominique anything. I wouldn't do that. But his next words have me snapping my mouth closed.

"Guess I was wrong. You're just as twisted and fucked up as his family is. No wonder you two get along. Birds of a feather…"

Fly together.

A stab of guilt pierces my chest. "I didn't say anything." My voice cracks.

Deacon's upper lip curls in disgust and he turns back to the front of the room.

"I'm serious. I wouldn't do that, I swear. He has no idea about you two, you know…"

He gives me a withering look.

"… being related."

Scrutinizing me with his gaze, I wait on pins and needles for his final verdict. I don't know how he figured out Dom was with me last night, but the more I think about it, the quicker I realize we didn't take any extra precautions.

I assumed I only had to worry about one of the other girls walking in on us or seeing him on his way out. As long as those two bases were covered, we were in the clear. At least, I thought we were.

"His ride was at your place all night," he said. "Parked right next to your Subaru."

Shit. That was stupid.

"It's not what you think."

"You've said that already."

Well, it seemed worth repeating.

"Why was he there? If you want me to believe you didn't call him over the second I left your place, answer me that."

The surrounding seats fill with the bodies of our classmates as the clock ticks closer to the start of class. He already thinks I'm sleeping with him. Might as well just admit to it already.

"He didn't come over until late. Like really late." I wiggle my brows, hoping he gets my meaning without making me say it out loud.

"Your point?"

He's not going to make this easy on me. Awesome. "And when a guy goes to a girl's place at an unreasonable hour, he's usually only there for one thing."

Come on, Deacon. You've called me out on it before. Put two and two together here.

I'm making every hint, hint, and wink, wink, expression that I can, and he's still looking at me like he's pissed and has no clue what I'm trying to suggest.

"We fucked," I hiss. "There. Happy?"

I adjust the hoodie around my neck, wishing I'd left my hair down to hide the heat creeping up my face.

"He showed up for a booty call? That's what you're telling me." He doesn't sound convinced but some of the cold has left his voice, so at least now I face the refrigerator version of Deacon instead of the freezer one.

"Sure. Yeah. We'll call it that."

The corners of his mouth twitch. "Is there something else you want to call it?"

Heat blooms across my face, making my cheeks burn with embarrassment. "Sex. You can just say we had sex. You know, like two consenting adults. It doesn't have to be some dirty thing."

"It's a booty call, Kasey. Booty calls are dirty."

I sigh. "Whatever." Slumping in my seat, I cross my arms over my chest. "Happy now? Are we good?"

He snorts. "Am I happy that you confirmed what I already knew, that you're boning that asshole? No. Can't say I'm happy about it. But," He shrugs. "We're good. As long as you swear you didn't—"

"I didn't! Promise." That was the last thing on my mind when we were...you know.

Deacon must see some kind of look on my face because he brings his fist to his mouth as he says, "*Damn*. It was that good?"

I lie forward and wrap my arms over my head, hiding from the mortification I will die from any minute now. "Stop," I groan.

"Is that why you look like you've had such an interesting morning? Did you stay up too late doing the nasty, nasty?"

Shoot me now. Seriously. And who says that word like that these days? *Gross.*

"I'm done talking to you," I mumble into my arms, loud enough for him to hear me. "You know I didn't sell you down the river, so let's leave it at that."

"How—"

I raise my head and glare. "Nope. No questions. You got what you wanted, and I am not giving you the details of my sex life."

Someone behind us snickers.

"Come on," Deacon whines. "Is he as much of an unfeeling bastard in the sack as he is in real life? I bet he's selfish too, huh? Makes you work for your—"

"Okay. That's enough. How about we talk about you instead?" Anything to get him off this topic of conversation.

"Oh, I'm great in bed. And I'm real good at eating—"

"Not that," I bite out. "You! Like life, or I don't know. Stuff. But not that. I don't need to know any of that."

Any shards of ice that were in his expression before are officially gone as a wide grin splits his face, his eyes now filled with mirth.

"Alright. Fine." He rolls his eyes. "You're no fun."

Well, at least we sorted all that out. I don't appreciate him jumping to conclusions before hearing me out, but I can't really blame him. It wasn't a good look on my part. I should probably leave it at that. Class is about to begin and we're still close to turbulent waters here, but sometimes you just have to risk it.

"You need to tell him."

"No," he deadpans, knowing who and what I'm referring to. "I don't"

"Yes, you do," I say, dropping my voice low. "He's your brother. He should know."

Deacon scoffs. "What he is, is an asshole. I'm good. Just because you've admitted you're sleeping with him doesn't mean I have to like the guy now. He has his life. I have mine. We'll leave it at that. Besides, I won't have to deal with him much longer."

My brows pull together. "What's that supposed to mean?"

Our professor walks in and for once, Deacon decides to be a studious college kid and pay attention. He ignores me most of the class. He's not still angry with me anymore, from what I can tell. He's just actually paying attention in class for once.

That's fine. I'll harass him about telling Dominique later. He can only push off the inevitable for so long.

Dominique would want to know, and I get the feeling that Deacon didn't randomly choose to enroll at Suncrest U. He came here for him. And I'm pretty sure I'm the one who fucked all of his plans up. Damn. I didn't think about it before now, but that has to be it, right? Deacon was going to tell him.

Their paths must have crossed over the summer because even freshman start the football season before the semester begins, but maybe he was taking his time. Working up to letting Dominique know, and then boom! Deacon runs into me.

And just like that, Dominique's asshole switch is flipped and any chance Deacon had of getting on Dom's good side is washed away.

"Fuck." I mutter the curse under my breath. Urgh. I'm such an idiot. Now I really have to fix things between them.

Dominique is the least friendly person that I know. Aside from me and the guys, he doesn't talk to anyone else. I've seen him stone-cold ignore people at parties who walk right up to him and say hello. Half the time he won't even acknowledge them, which makes it awkward as hell if you're around to see it. It can take a minute or two for people to realize that no matter what they say or how many times they repeat themselves, he's not going to respond. Eventually, they get the hint, but it can take a while.

The other half of the time, he barks out an order to *go the fuck away*, and whoever it was that bothered him scurries off like a dog with their tail tucked between their legs. Saying Dominique's social skills are lacking is the understatement of the year. I don't know why he's like that. He used to ignore me, too. When I was a kid. He and the guys would come over to our place to hangout with Aaron. They were in middle school and I was still in elementary, but I remember trying to talk to him. I showed him my new basketball and asked if he wanted to shoot some hoops and he just stared. It was as though he could see through me. Like I didn't even exist.

I remember being so upset about it. Since then, I've gone out of my way to get under his skin. Anything to provoke a response and as I've gotten older,I've gotten really good at it. But Deacon doesn't know what Dominique is like. All he knew was that he had a brother out there he didn't know.

Was he excited when he got accepted to Suncrest U? When he joined the football team? And how disappointed was he when none of his plans went his way?

I wonder how many times he tried to strike up a conversation with Dom, and how many times it failed. That had to be rough. Picturing Dominique's responses in my head, it's no wonder Deacon won't tell him the truth. I probably wouldn't either.

FIFTEEN

DOMINIQUE

The week speeds past in a blur, not bothering to slow down when it hits the weekend before bulldozing into the next week. It's Friday now. *Fuck.* Already? A quick look at my phone confirms. Not going to lie, I'm a little surprised to see I was right.

I rarely know what day of the week it is anymore. I'm still hitting PT at the ass crack of dawn before practice in the mornings. That runs until 9 a.m. most days. Sometimes 10 a.m.

Next week it won't be as bad. I got the all clear on my shoulder, so I'm good to go. No need to take things easy on the field or in practice anymore.

About fucking time. I could've used those extra hours to catch up on sleep since as soon as practice lets out, I have just enough time for a shower and a bite to eat before my classes pick up in the afternoon. Throw in trying to babysit Aaron without letting him on to the fact that I'm keeping an eye on him, and any free time I might have is eliminated.

The guy's been all over the place lately. Some days he's so out of it he sleeps all day or binge watches TV for eight hours straight. And the other days he's an ADHD kid who skipped his meds, pinging all over the place.

He has an official diagnosis and doesn't medicate. Addict problems. What can you do?

Since he only takes classes part-time, his ADHD isn't normally this recognizable, but the other day, he came home with something like twenty canvases, an easel, and five separate acrylic paint sets. Not five individual colors. Full on fucking collections of the entire rainbow. And something like twenty-five paint brushes, most of which are the same size and shape but came in a different color which meant he needed one of each.

In the years I've known him, he has never had a creative bone in his body. The guy can weld and that's about it. But drawing or painting or anything like that, he's never had an interest. Now, he does.

Which was fine until three hours of listening to music and painting his heart out went by and he abandoned all of his shit in our living room to reorganize every cabinet and drawer we have in the kitchen instead.

He spent two hours on that and was pretty fucking proud of himself afterwards. Again, fine. I'll survive not knowing where the hell anything is. It's whatever.

But it didn't stop there. Aaron was so proud of his organizational skills, he decided to organize the entire fucking house, in the middle of the night no less.

The team weight trains in the evenings, giving me even less time or, trust me, I would have put a stop to this. But I didn't know what that shithead was up to until the next morning when I showed up at 3 a.m. to find him wide awake, and all of our belongings strewn across the floor while he *organized*.

It was a disaster.

The only upside is that he was so distracted he didn't think to ask me where I'd been or why I was home so late. But that's the one and only upside.

Two days later, our place is still a disaster. Aaron was hyper fixated for a few hours sorting through shit, only for his motivation to run dry around the time I got home. This guy kills me. I'm telling you, I do not know how I put up with this shit. If my hair turns gray in my twenties, it'll be because of him.

I'm giving him the weekend while I'm away to get it figured out before calling a professional organizer and a maid to get it handled.

We have a housekeeper already, but she only comes once a month to deep clean the place. I'm a grown fucking adult. I can do my laundry and clean up after myself just fine, not that anyone would know that with what my place looks like right now. But I take care of my responsibilities.

And the only reason I have a housekeeper at all is because my parents fired Rhea for missing a few crumbs on the kitchen counter when she'd been working for them for nine years. I've spent more meaningful time with her than I have with my own parents, which is how I know she's got kids and grandkids who rely on her income.

I cover what she used to make working for my parents, but I only let her come once a week instead of the five days she'd work for them. She's insisted on helping more, but we don't need it and I won't cut her pay when my parents are assholes who fired her in the first place. She doesn't deserve to be shit on, and I won't have her show up next week, expecting her usual workload, and find the shit storm Aaron created instead.

Fucking hell. At least everything else in my life isn't a disaster.

Hookups with Kasey are still a regular thing, and the only reason I'm sane. Things shifted between us after I took another of her firsts. I've tried not to read into it, but on today of all days, when I'm supposed to leave town, it's all I've thought about besides Aaron and his bullshit.

Before when Kasey and I would fuck, there was this cloud of despair hanging around her. She'd lost some of her spark and you could see the demons she fought against every time you looked into her gaze.

When I'd buried myself inside her, she wasn't fully present. I doubt she could afford to be. Sex was her outlet and when she came to me for pleasure, for an escape, she used it to push back her demons, locking pieces of herself away, so she had the strength of will to fight for another day.

That's not what I see when I'm inside her anymore.

That cloud of despair has lifted. Or maybe it's just harder for me to tell now with Aaron around. She spent more time at the house when he was gone, so I saw the shifts in her mood and knew when she was bending too far, getting ready to break.

I only see brief flashes of her now when she swings by to visit her brother, and it's always in passing. She doesn't linger long after I get home, making it hard to get a read on her moods.

And later, when I sneak into her room at night, there's only one thing on either of our minds and we spend most of the night doing it. We don't talk. Not unless I'm telling her how good she is at taking my cock, or she's begging me for more. But I think I've figured out what happened. Why things don't feel the same between us anymore.

Kasey doesn't need me to fuck her grief out of her anymore. She doesn't need help keeping her demons at bay.

What I still haven't figured out though is that if she doesn't need me for her grief anymore, why does she message me every night asking when I'll come over? And once I'm there, why does she sometimes say things like, *I wish you could stay?*

SIXTEEN
KASEY

I'm walking back to the Kappa Mu house after class when someone shouts, "Hey! Wait up."

I look around me, but don't see anyone to go with the voice. Shrugging, I keep walking. Cutting through one of the parking lots, I'm almost to Greek Row when they call again.

"Kasey! Hold up!"

Okay, that was definitely for me. Stopping, I lift my hand to my face, blocking the sun from my eyes, and spin in a slow circle, looking for the speaker.

Firm hands grip my hips, turning me around. "Hey!" Striking out, I shove whoever it is touching me hard in the chest. He grunts and takes a second longer before letting go.

Taking two steps away, I blink back against the sun as it tries to blind me and take in the body that belongs to the voice. "Thanks a lot, Satan. You almost gave me a heart attack."

Dominique's mouth twitches, fighting back a grin. "We're back to Satan, are we?"

I shrug. "Once a devil, always a devil."

This time, the smile breaks free, accompanied by a bark of laughter. "I couldn't have scared you," he says. "I called your name twice. You avoiding me, now? Is there something I should know about?" His voice is teasing and he closes the small distance I put between us.

"No. I didn't know it was you, and I'm late to help Quinn decorate for a party." Turning, I head for my place and Dominique easily falls into step beside me, his longer strikes moving at a much more relaxed pace.

"What party?"

The one I intentionally did not mention because of the way you acted at the last one. He humiliated me in front of everyone, ordering me out of the swimming pool because my swimsuit was *indecent.*

For reference, it was. But who the hell cares? It's a swimsuit. It covered all of my important bits and I looked great.

I'll rock the shit out of that suit every chance I get, just to see the vein on Dominique's forehead pulse the way it did that day, seconds away from exploding. I don't think I've ever seen him so angry in my life than he was at every single guy who was there, all because they looked at me.

Dominique is allergic to all things Greek. I'm not a fan of the fraternity and sorority lifestyle, but I've gotten used to it since classes began. It's not great. But it's better than I expected it to be, so I won't complain. And while I've learned to tolerate Greek Row, Dom hates it. It's not because of the parties, I don't think. But the entitlement and inflated egos. Not that he's one to talk.

"Party isn't the right word," I hedge.

Tucking his hands in his pockets, he gives me a look that says, *I don't believe you.* "What word would you use, then?"

Hmm... the one that won't back me into a corner.

"It's a get together. You know how the girls are at Kappa Mu. To them, even four friends constitute calling it a party. Makes it sound more exciting than it is."

Pressing his tongue to his cheek, he nods, but his forehead creases, showing he's not ready to let this go. "When is it?"

"When is what?" I chirp and even throw in some batting of my eyelashes. Not that it does me any good.

A low growl rises in his throat. "Don't play dumb."

I exhale a loud breath. "I don't know why you're getting worked up about this. It's the girls doing the shit they always do. No big deal and zero reason to get all snarly with me about it."

A muscle pulses in his neck. "When?" he demands.

Urgh. Fine. "Later tonight. Happy now?"

His jaw ticks. That would be a no.

"You're going?"

"I do live there," I remind him with a shrug. "But I figure you'll come over tonight, so I'll be around until you show up. Quinn won't let me out of it." She knows about Mom and has given me space, but according to her, the time for space is over and I'm being dragged back into the fold.

"I'll hang out for an hour or two at most before you come over." I didn't invite him. Not that it matters. Dominique is Suncrest U's quarterback. Formal invitation or not, he's welcomed with open arms at every party or social gathering on campus.

Hell, the same rule probably applies to everything that goes on in Sun Valley. If not because of his position on the team, then because of his family name. There are perks to being a Price.

If Dominique wants to show up, he'll show up. My feelings on the matter won't stop him.

"I won't be there."

My shoulders dip in relief. "Great."

Dominique responds to my comment with a dark scowl. *Whoops.* Could have kept that last statement to myself.

"Not just the party," he adds, not missing a step. "I won't be at your place tonight. Or this weekend."

I stumble before catching myself. *Oh.* My shoulders droop for a different reason now. Whatever. It's fine. I've seen him every day for weeks. We could use some space. I mean, yeah. Of course we could.

It's never long before I reach the top of my *Tolerance for Dominique* meter anyway, so this is perfect timing. If he leaves now, it'll make it easier to deal with him later.

Forcing myself to smile through the disappointment I refuse to acknowledge right now, I force out a casual, "Busy?"

He nods. "I have a game in Richland tomorrow. Most of the team is heading out tonight and I'm driving Roman and Emilio."

I knew he had a game coming up. I just didn't know it was coming up this soon.

"Fun. I'm sure you guys will do great."

"Thanks," he grunts.

And cue the end of that conversation. I sigh. Dominique walks beside me the rest of the way home, though I'm not sure why. His car is probably back on campus near the football stadium so he'll have to walk back and grab it before going home.

Ten minutes of silent walking later and we've reached the side entrance to Kappa Mu. "Well, this was fun." I rock back on my feet. "Guess I'll see you—"

"Tuesday."

I lift both of my brows. "Tuesday?" I ask, not sure if I heard him right. Why wouldn't I see him until Tuesday when he just said the game was on Saturday?

"A few things came up."

Like? I wait for him to fill me in, but he doesn't.

"O-kay. Well, bye."

He's not leaving and I haven't opened the door. I don't know what he's waiting for. Does he expect a goodbye kiss, or maybe a hug?

We don't do that sort of thing. I mean, we kiss plenty but the, *I want to devour you,* kisses. Not the sweet, *I'm going to miss you,* ones.

Is that what he wants? Considering it, I step closer and hesitate for only a second before leaning up onto the tips of my toes and placing a quick kiss on his warm, brown cheek. Dropping back to my feet, I look up to see his eyes flash with surprise. Oh crap.

I reach for the door, eager for a hasty retreat. Based on that quick glimpse of shock on his face, I'd say he was not waiting for a goodbye kiss and I just made a fool of myself.

"See you around." The heat of embarrassment prickles my skin and I jerk open the door, wishing I could disappear.

"Yeah, I'll uh," he stammers, and that just makes it ten times weirder because when the hell has Dominique Price ever stammered? I must have really thrown him for a loop there. "See you around."

With a backward wave, he walks back in the direction we came from as I step inside the Kappa Mu house, closing it behind me. Why did I kiss him on the cheek? He isn't my boyfriend or some soldier leaving for war. He'll be gone for the weekend, which is normal. It's not like he'll miss me. I won't miss him.

When he gets back, everything will go back to the way it was.

I groan and press my fingers to my eyelids. Kissing him made things weird. Why did I do that? I'm an idiot.

What happens if Dominique comes back and realizes he doesn't want things back how they were? Or worse, that he does, but not to the way they were before he left for the game. What if he decides we should go all the way back to the way it was before we slept together? When I was just Aaron's little sister and he was nothing more than my older brother's infuriating best friend?

SEVENTEEN
DOMINIQUE

"Yes. I know," I tell Coach, half listening to him as I walk to the edge of the street. Looking to my left, then to my right, I jog across the four lane street and head for the entrance to La Dour. The restaurant I'm meeting Andres DeAnde at. I'm not late, but I will be if Coach doesn't stop his fussing so I can hang up and go inside.

"I've got it. Relax. I'm here."

He continues with his tirade of advice, but I tuned most of him out fifteen minutes ago. It's mostly the same three pieces of advice he's given me at least a dozen times since we arrived in Richland three days ago.

Hear the man out.

Don't say no to any offers until I have the chance to sleep on it.

Don't be an asshole.

Simple enough. I met Andres briefly at the game so I know who to look for when I step inside the restaurant. He stopped by to scope out the team, I guess. Said hi to Roman, calling him by his first name. Roman acted like they knew each other, which was weird, but I couldn't ask him about it with DeAnde standing right there, and I didn't have time to question him during the game.

After we won, he and Emilio hitched a ride back with the rest of the team, eager to get back to their women, and I checked into my hotel. Alone. It sucked.

"Yeah. Uh, huh."

I don't hear what he says, but my noncommittal responses have dragged this conversation out long enough.

"I'm hanging up now," I tell him before ending the call. Tucking the phone into the pocket of my suit jacket, I take a deep breath and open the door.

Right away, the scent of garlic and herbs hits my senses. When I looked it up online, La Dour was listed as Richland's premier French restaurant. A bit too on the nose if you ask me.

But who knows, it could be a coincidence that he picked a French restaurant without knowing I was born and spent the first six years of my life living in France.

Giving my name to the hostess, she leads me to a table in the far corner of the room where Andres DeAnde already sits with a glass of amber liquid. He raises it toward me before bringing it to his mouth.

"You made it," he says, taking a drink before tilting his glass toward the hostess, indicating he'd like another.

"I'll have your server bring one over," she says to him before turning to me. "Can I get you a—"

"Water is fine," I say.

Unbuttoning my suit jacket, I take the seat across from DeAnde and wait to hear what he has to say. He doesn't leave me waiting long and gets straight to the point.

"You're a good quarterback."

"Thank you." Leaning back, I wait. If he expects me to gush like some school girl over his praises, he has the wrong guy. I know I'm a good quarterback. Outside affirmations aren't really my thing.

"Good enough to play pro."

I nod. Again, he isn't telling me anything I don't know.

"Your Coach tells me you're not planning to enter the draft."

Our server arrives with his drink and my water and we pause long enough to place our orders. *Coq au vin*, for him and the *Confit de canard*, for me. As soon as she takes our menus and steps away, he continues.

"Is there a reason for that?"

"I'm a junior." But I'm sure he knows that already. "And my father has aspirations for me to join the family business."

He smiles. It's almost... unnerving.

There are few people in the world capable of intimidating me, and I'm beginning to suspect that Andres DeAnde might be one of them. There are rumors surrounding how he's amassed his fortune. You need money from the start to purchase a football team, so the team isn't his money maker. My guess, it's his hobby. It's that way for most owners. You reach a certain point where you have more cash than you can spend in your lifetime. I would know. My family is there. Only my father has no interest in athletics. DeAnde does.

"Ah, yes," he says. "Richard has always been a man consumed by legacy."

My brows shoot up to my hairline and I give Andres a calculated look. Dressed in a black suit with a black button-down shirt, he could easily pass for a business man until he turns his face, exposing the top of his neck where the dark edges of a tattoo attempt to hide. Interesting. Searching for more details, I note the signet ring on his right hand and the wedding band on his left. He's married to a former business rival's daughter if I remember right. Wonder how that's working out for him.

His dark brown hair is slicked back from his face. His jaw freshly shaved. He knows what he's doing, and the look is passable. But there's an edge to the way he carries himself, one you don't achieve by spending time in country clubs and boardrooms, which are the only places I can imagine he'd get the chance to cross paths with my father.

"You two know each other?" I raise the glass of water to my lips.

"We do," is his only response.

This is a test. DeAnde stokes my curiosity while figuring out what I know. If they do know each other, he might wonder if my father has mentioned him before. What opinions I have that are already formed. I'm young, but I'm not stupid. I won't bite at the first carrot he dangles in front of my face.

Amused, he shifts to more comfortable topics and shortly after, our server arrives with our food. We eat our meal in silence, offering the occasional thought or compliment on the food. The silence isn't uncomfortable. He appears to enjoy small talk as much as I do.

When our server returns to clear our plates, we both decline a look at the dessert menu and Andres orders himself a third drink.

"Are you sure you don't want one?" he asks. "You're of age. I'm not going to judge you for a single indulgence."

"Thanks, but I'm good." And I don't give two shits about his judgments.

"Very well. Onto business, then?"

I nod, eager to get this meeting over with. I appreciate Coach for setting it up. He's looking out for me. But at the end of the day, this is just a waste of time.

"I want you on my team."

"Funny," I deadpan.

"Is it?" he asks, the edge from earlier entering his voice.

Neither one of us is laughing.

"Why?"

"I told you already. You're a good quarterback."

Not good enough. "Hector Rayes is better, and you already have him."

"He could be traded to a different team."

"Is that what's happening?" I ask, lifting one brow.

His lips twitch with the hint of a smile. "No."

Didn't think so.

"From where I sit, it doesn't look like you need another QB for your team."

"Perhaps." His eyes bore into mine when he says "But I want you. You won't start. Most first years don't, but you have the potential to get there if you leave your ego off my field."

Not a problem, but I keep my words to myself. "Appreciate it, but like I said, I'm only a junior. I have a year left of school and a different path I intend to follow."

"What if I told you that I can't be bought by your father nor can I be bribed?"

I lean back in my seat. This just got interesting. "I'm listening."

"I went to school with your father. We both graduated from All Souls Academy when we were kids. Did he ever tell you?"

I shake my head. My father doesn't talk to me about his life, he just tries to control mine.

"We were rivals as children, even more so when we went to college. Over the years, our paths have crossed a number of times and when they do, we tend to give one another a wide berth. It's been an unspoken rule between us for longer than I can remember. He has his empire and I have mine."

A sinking clarity washes over me. "What did he do?"

Andres' grin is feral. "He stuck his nose where it didn't belong. And I'd like to return the favor."

"By offering his son an easy path to the big leagues?" I scoff. "I doubt that."

"There are two things Richard Price considers so far beneath him that no child of his can ever pursue them Music and Sports. He'd want you to work as a bag boy in a supermarket before you ever got a career in either field. Am I right?"

He's not wrong.

"All my years growing up with your father gave me a look into that twisted yet brilliant mind of his. He refuses to see his name associated with African American stereotypes of success and he is vehemently determined to see his legacy thrive. If you play for me, I cut both of his legs out from under him. So you see, my offer makes perfect sense."

"And admitting all of this should convince me to take you up on your offer? You expect me to drop out of college and risk my father's wrath, quite possibly getting disowned, to satisfy your need for revenge for an offense my father made that I don't even know the details of?"

"Yes."

I bark out a laugh. Guess we made that clear.

"You're insane."

"And you want a career in football. Tell me I'm wrong."

Jaw clenched, I grind my molars together. "I know the way his mind works. He can buy off anyone else. You will never play professional football."

I grunt. "I'm aware."

"Unless you come and play for me."

EIGHTEEN
KASEY

The next three days suck.

Quinn forces me to attend the party Friday night, but I outright refuse to stick around for the one the girls throw together at the last minute on Saturday. One party full of drunk college students who like to grope each other on our couch is more than enough for me.

I spend most of Saturday by myself in my room, doing homework and submitting some of my makeup assignments. I still have a lot of ground to cover, but the time alone at least puts a dent in my workload.

On Sunday, boredom gets the better of me and I give Aaron a call to see if he wants to meet up.

He does. Only now that I'm here, I don't know if this was a great idea.

We're in the living room, Mom's ashes in an urn between us.

"So?" I've got nothing.

Aaron sighs and runs his hands through his shaggy blond hair. "Sorry. Didn't mean to spring this on you."

"It's fine." Sort of. I mean, I knew mom was cremated, but I didn't prepare myself for the realization that this was all we had left of her.

"Do you still want to spread her ashes at Myrtle Bay?"

Right. That'd been my original suggestion. Swallowing hard, I nod. "Yeah. I think she'd like that."

Neither one of us says anything after that, we just stare at her cremated remains and, like a dam forced to contain too much pressure, I crack.

"I miss her." I suck in a shuddering breath.

Aaron lifts his eyes to me, letting me see the tears he's fighting to contain.

"Yeah." He sniffs. "Me too."

Like two magnets, we move toward one another and I bury my nose in his chest. Aaron wraps his arms around me while I wind mine around his waist, my shoulders shaking.

"It's not fair," I whisper.

He presses his cheek to the side of my head and his wet tears fall down his face and onto my skin. "I know," he tells me. "I know."

We say nothing after that. There isn't a need to. Aaron holds me while I cry, and I do the same for him in return. It's cathartic in a way. I thought I'd gotten all of my tears out before, but I guess there were more hiding in there.

When the silence breaks with the sound of our rumbling stomachs, we break apart with a laugh, wipe our faces clean, and go out to get some food.

We grab burgers at Sun Valley Station before going back to his place for a movie marathon and binge watch Game of Thrones. We make it through the first season, but call it quits before starting the second, and I stay the night in his guest bedroom, needing to be close to my brother.

The next morning I go to class like usual, but we meet again for lunch, and when he finishes his afternoon classes, we resume our marathon and dive into season two.

Aaron's phone buzzes around five and I catch sight of Dominique's name flashing across the screen. Aaron doesn't mention what the messages say as they text back and forth several times during the show, and I have too much pride to bother asking.

I haven't spoken to him since Friday when he said he'd be gone. I've thought about it, sure. I could call him or even shoot him a message, but why would I? He hasn't bothered to reach out to me, so I assume he's busy. That, or disinterested.

I pretend that he's busy. I haven't let myself think too much about him while he's been away. Or worry about what will happen once he returns.

Around episode three of season two, Aaron pauses the show. "I have to run out for a bit," he says. "Pick this up in a few hours?"

"Sure," I tell him with a smile. "Not like I have anything better to do."

He chuckles and grabs his wallet and keys from the coffee table. "Thanks, sis."

"Anytime." I fold the blanket I'd been using and lay it over the back of the sofa.

"You don't have to leave," he tells me. "You can hangout and nap or whatever."

"Nap?" I ask, lifting my brows.

"What? Naps are awesome. And don't pretend you weren't about to doze there on the couch."

He's got me there. "Sure." I give my brother a wink. "I'll take over your guest room while you do whatever you need to. Wake me up when you get back?"

"You got it."

I wake up from my nap and rub the sleep from my face before stepping into the living room to see if Aaron is back, but instead of finding my brother, it's Dominique who's returned.

He stands next to the window, dressed to the nines in a dark gray suit.

Woah.

My mouth goes dry. I don't think I've ever seen Dominique dressed up like this. Not in person, at least. His pants are a dark charcoal gray, the seams pressed into tight, crisp lines down his legs. He's paired it with a black, button-down shirt and a gray vest. His tie is another shade of gray, a little lighter and with a sheen. It's wrapped in an intricate knot at his throat. Not one of those simple two-second styles you see guys wear to prom or a wedding. This one has layers and folds and somehow makes Dominique appear more mature. Almost regal. Like he's someone to take seriously.

An expensive-looking tie clip glints in the low light, studded with tiny stones I know have to be real. A glance at his wrists shows an equally expensive pair of cufflinks. Monogrammed with his initials. *D.P.*

I ignore the inappropriate thought that pops into my head and scan the rest of the room, spotting the suit jacket draped elegantly over the back of the sofa. Looks like he's pulled out all the stops.

Dominique keeps his gaze trained out the window, hands shoved in his pockets like he's waiting for someone to arrive. Who could it be?

"Going somewhere?" I ask and step out from the hallway.

His head jerks up and an almost guilty expression flickers across his face before he masks it. "The team has this thing tonight." He waves a hand dismissively through the air. "A charity dinner I have to go to."

Oh. Realization dawns on me. "The McIntire dinner?"

His dark brown gaze flicks to mine and he adjusts his cufflinks. "Yeah. Didn't think you'd know about that."

I swallow past the lump in my throat and plaster on a fake smile. "Some of the Kappa Mu girls are going with players on the team," I tell him and force out a laugh. "Quinn ran all over the house getting ready today."

It's all she's been talking about this week. How excited she is to go. What a big deal being invited to the McIntire dinner is. I guess a lot of snooty business execs will be there, so it's as much of a networking opportunity as it is a social event.

Dom grunts, but doesn't comment, and I wrack my brain for any details Quinn might have mentioned. I didn't pay close attention when she talked about it. I know one of the defensive lineman asked her to go. She said something about every team member getting an extra ticket to bring a plus one. It's why the girls threw so many parties this past week. They wanted as many chances to show off for the players as they could get to land one of the coveted plus one seats.

The McIntire dinner is a big deal to a lot of people on campus, and tickets for attendees—outside of the team who are obligated to attend—are expensive. Something like five-hundred dollars per person since it's a boujie charity thing. But every guy on the team gets a plus one. That's what Quinn said.

Dominique never mentioned it and he didn't ask me to go with him, which means he's taking somebody else as his date. A stab of hurt slams into my chest and I shove it away.

What do I care? I would have said no, anyway. Formal dinners aren't my scene, and it's not like we're dating. *It's just sex,* I remind myself. But the blooming ache just beneath my ribs disagrees with me.

Chewing my bottom lip, I ignore the needles pricking the backs of my eyes and repeat all the reasons this shouldn't matter in my head.

We are not a thing. We aren't dating. We're fuck buddies and sort of friends and Dominique doesn't owe me anything. Our relationship, if you can even call it that, is a secret. Going out together, on a public date of all things, to a fancy event where a bunch of people we know will be, would blow our situation out of the water.

That's why he didn't ask me. He couldn't. There's no reason to feel blindsided.

Dom always has a date at these things and as far as I know, it's always been the same woman on his arm.

There's a knock at the door before it swings open and a woman I vaguely recognize pokes her head inside. "Knock knock."

Her.

Tamara steps into the room and I suck in a sharp breath. She's even prettier in person. The stupid high school girl inside of me hates her straight away. We've never met. I've only ever seen her in pictures. And if I see another one of her again, I am going to viciously X out her face or tear off her head before throwing the damn thing away.

"Are you all set?" she asks, her attention solely focused on Dominique. And just, *wow.* Does she have to be so pretty? She's petite, around my height, but a hell of a lot curvier in all the ways men appreciate. She has a large chest. A full D cup at least, and her cleavage is off the charts. Even I can't stop staring at it.

She's wearing a figure hugging, white dress that stops just below her thighs, a few inches shy of indecent. The shimmery material contrasts with her rich dark skin and highlights her thin waist, flared hips, and toned thighs. Her dark brown locs are twisted into an elegant bun with a few jeweled pins added as embellishments, and she's wearing strappy, white stilettos that I would one-hundred percent fall flat on my face in.

Her legs are long and lean despite her small stature, so basically, she looks amazing. And here I am in a pair of leggings and an oversized t-shirt with my hair haphazardly thrown into a messy bun, half of which has fallen out of my scrunchy and hangs in loose curls around my face.

How the hell am I supposed to compete with that?

I can't.

She hasn't noticed I'm here. I'm all but invisible with the way she and Dominique look at one another. Like they're eager to leave. To be alone.

"Yeah," Dom grunts, and retrieves his jacket from the sofa before moving for the door.

He's about to leave and something dark and vicious swirls in my stomach, making bile rise in my throat as he places his hand on the small of Tamara's back. Dominique pauses just outside the door and turns to look at me over his shoulder.

"I'll uh," His throat works to swallow, his discomfort obvious as he says, "I'll see you later." The question in his gaze surprises me.

Is that what he thinks? That he'll go out with a girl like that and still show up at my room later tonight?

When I don't respond, he adds, "Coach will have my balls if I try to bail, but Aaron should be back soon. Do you need us to wait until he gets here?" He glances at the clock. It's obvious he doesn't have time to wait. Not that I want him to. Gah. Can you imagine? The three of us awkwardly sitting in the living room until my brother gets home?

No, thank you. This was bad enough.

I wave him off, shoving down the emotions that clog my throat. Screw him. Deacon was right. Dominique is having his cake and eating it, too.

Tamara's been on his arm at every major Suncrest U event since Dom's freshman year. I'm an idiot, and I should have seen this coming. She's endgame material. He wouldn't keep her around if there wasn't something there. I made a mistake thinking that because I never saw her around, she wasn't important. I was wrong. My chest burns like someone is pressing hot coals to it. I can't drag enough air into my lungs, but I somehow manage to force out one word.

"Nope." I blink hard and cough to clear my throat. "Have fun."

Dom's mouth twists into a grimace. I don't sound convincing, but what does he expect me to say? Yes. Stay with me, but make her go away? Skip dinner or take me instead?

It'd never happen, and even if it would, I'm not desperate enough to ask. Forcing a smile, I pretend everything is okay.

Dominique Price is a free man. He can go on dates with whoever he wants without talking to me or considering my feelings about it. We're not in a relationship. What we have is an arrangement.

As long as he doesn't sleep with her, he's not breaking the rules. The reminder should offer some level of comfort, but it doesn't. We agreed not to sleep around with other people, but what if he changes his mind? How would I even know?

And there's a lot two people can do outside of explicit sex. The thought shoots ice into my veins.

Look at her. Of course, he'd want to screw around with her. Who wouldn't? I'm not into girls and even I'd consider experimenting if it was with someone who looked like that.

Will he tell me before it happens? Should I expect a late night message from Dominique letting me know the deal is off and that he's fucking her instead? Maybe he'll fill me in after it happens. A belated courtesy if he gives me one at all. *Fuck.* I'm going to be sick.

Tamara watches our exchange before meeting my gaze. Her head tilts to the side, almond eyes openly curious. "Oh. Hi," she says with a laugh. "I didn't see you there. I'm Tamara."

I give her a small wave because what else am I supposed to do here? "Kasey. Nice to meet you."

"You too. Do you live here too, with..." she trails off, leaving me to fill in the blanks as she looks at Dom, expecting one of us to answer.

She's good, I'll give her that. With one question, she can determine our situation without being obnoxiously obvious about it. Only curious.

"No." Dominique doesn't elaborate, but my nerves force me to fill the silence.

"Aaron is my brother," I tell her, realizing I gave her the answer she wanted, confirming I'm no one to Dominique.

Pointing down the hallway, I take a few retreating steps. "I forgot a few things in the guest room." Screw waiting for my brother to get home. I need to get out of here. "But it was nice meeting you." *Not.*

Dominique looks at me like I'm acting weird, but I ignore him and make my escape, turning the corner to the hallway before pressing my back to the wall and sucking in a desperate breath.

Tamara says something to him I can't make out. But Dominique's voice is deep, allowing me to hear his reply.

"No. There's nothing between us," he tells her, and my heart plummets to the pit of my stomach. Nope. Nothing at all. Swallowing hard, I push away from the wall and force my feet to move to the guest bedroom as my heart splinters, pieces of it falling onto the wooden floor.

It takes everything in me not to slam the bedroom door once I'm inside, but I make myself slow down, taking a deep breath and closing it with infinite care before I slump against it.

The front door closes, signaling that they've left, and I slide to the floor, pulling my legs to my chest and wrapping my arms around my knees before burying my face.

Deacon warned me this would happen. That I'd get hurt. And he was right. This fucking hurts. So goddamn much.

I should have listened to him when he told me to end it. It still would've hurt, but I'd at least have my pride. I wouldn't be sitting here, pining for Dominique like a pathetic school girl while he goes on a date with another woman.

My heart races in my chest and the edge of panic sinks down my spine. I will not fall apart because of him. No way. He does not get to have that kind of power over me.

Wiping my eyes, I grab my phone and keys, waiting just long enough to assure myself that Dominique and Tamara are gone.

I use the short drive back to the Kappa Mu house to clear my head. I need a distraction. Something to do that will keep me from thinking about what the two of them are doing, but as soon as I step inside the house, I know this isn't where I'll find one.

"Hello?" I call out into the empty living room.

Silence greets me.

Looks like Quinn wasn't the only one who landed a plus one spot.

I climb the stairs to the second floor before knocking on a few of the other girls' doors just to be sure. I never come up here. Aside from Quinn, I don't talk to anyone else, not unless I have to. Every one of my knocks is greeted with silence. There are twelve of us living here. And tonight of all nights, I'm the only one alone.

Swallowing hard, I go back downstairs and head for my room. As soon as I step inside, my phone chimes with a message alert and I jump at the chance for a distraction.

Pulling it from my back pocket, I see Deacon's name illuminated on the screen.

Deacon: Who TF is this chick?

THERE'S AN ATTACHMENT. Clicking on it, it opens to reveal a close-up image of Dominique and his date. Lovely. Pressing my lips together, I stare at them together. Tamara looks good on his arm. Like she belongs there.

I fucking hate it.

It takes my shaking hands three attempts to type out a response. One that won't make me sound like a jilted lover.

Me: Her name is Tamara Vinzent. She's pretty.

UNDERSTATEMENT OF THE YEAR.

Deacon: I don't give a shit what her name is. Why is she on Price's arm instead of you?

TEARS PRICK the backs of my eyes, but I blink them away. I will not cry over a boy. Mom taught me better than that.

Me: *shrug emoji* You'd have to ask him.

Deacon: He didn't show up because you turned him down?

Me: Nope.

THAT I WASN'T INVITED IS IMPLIED.

My phone jumps in my hand, the vibration of an incoming call startling me before I see Deacon's name flash across the screen.

I answer it on the first ring and before I can even say hello he bites out a harsh, "Where are you?"

"Kappu Mu. Why?"

"Do you have a dress?"

I frown, glancing at my closet.

"What?"

"A dress. Do you have a dress? Something formal."

"Uh, yeah. I think so —" I don't have a lot of reasons to dress up, but even I have a little black dress. Mom says they're a staple, and when I turned sixteen, she bought me one. I've been the same size since freshman year, so I know it still fits.

"Good. Get ready. I'll be there in fifteen."

Wait. What? "What do you mean you'll be here in fifteen minutes? You're on the team, too. Don't you have to be at the McIntire dinner? You can't just leave."

He curses under his breath. "Kasey, there is no way in hell I'm going to stand around at this bullshit dinner while you're home alone and this idiot is parading around with some other chick."

An uncomfortable ache stabs me in my chest.

"Get ready. I'm picking you up, and that asshole can eat crow when he sees you as my date."

"Slow down," I sputter. "That is a terrible idea." Not that I wouldn't love to see the look on Dominique's face when I show up on Deacon's arm, but he has to know this will come back and bite him in the ass. "We only recently got you out of his line of fire, remember? And besides, don't you have a date?"

"I don't care, and no, I don't have a date," he says, taking me by surprise. "Me and a few of the guys came stag to chill with one another."

"Why?" The girls here throw themselves at football players left and right and Deacon, despite being a freshman, gets just as much attention as the upperclassmen. He could have had his choice of dates.

With an annoyed huff, he says, "Because I figured the one chick I'd want to bring was spoken for. Turns out, I was wrong."

Oh.

I swallow hard and think about it. Like seriously think about it. It's immature of me to go only to what, make Dominique jealous? I'd be taking advantage of Deacon's kindness for petty revenge, assuming it would even work.

"He's your brother," I remind him. If he wants to have a relationship with Dom, I can't keep getting in the way. "Do you want to risk pissing him off?"

I'm not deluded into thinking Dominique will see me there and realize he has feelings for me like some storybook fairytale. He's made his intentions clear. But he is possessive, and something about Deacon gets under his skin.

Me being there won't bother him for the right reasons. But it will piss him off. It's enough. But only if Deacon knows what he's getting himself into. What he's putting at risk.

"He's not my brother. He's just some asshole who shares half my DNA and, frankly, the fucker needs to learn a lesson."

"Okay. I'll get ready." Dread mixed with anticipation prickles against my skin.

"Good. I'm already on my way. You've got twelve minutes, sweetheart. Tick tock."

TWENTY

DOMINIQUE

W e've been here less than an hour and already I want to leave. Clustered beside me are my mother, sister, and two women I don't know, but who are clearly important to my mother. Tamara speaks with them, playing her part as the doting girlfriend with her hand on my arm as she laughs at something one of the woman says and keeps their attention, ensuring I'm left the fuck alone.

I hate things like this. The forced small talk and the fake smiles. I've had enough, but we'll have to endure at least an hour or two more.

"Spring would be lovely," my mother coos. "Don't you think?"

There's a lull in conversation and I realize my mother is waiting for an answer. "Spring?" What is she going on about?

"For the wedding," my mother says.

"We haven't—" Tamara says, but my mother steamrolls right over her. Politely, of course. Sheridan Price is well versed in social etiquette, so you wouldn't know that her shrill laugh is how she cuts people off, paving the way for her to interject.

"Yes, dear, I know. But it's been three years. Don't let him fool you. Dominique has something in mind, don't you dear."

Grinding my teeth, I give a shrug, ignoring how uncomfortable her statement makes me.

"You know how these Price men can be," she stage whispers. "They like their surprises."

My father has never surprised my mother with anything.

I grunt, taking a drink from the glass of water in my hand, wishing it was something stronger. I catch Roman's gaze across the room. His eyes flicker to the company around me and he raises his glass to me with a grimace.

Good luck.

I need it.

I block out my mother's voice as I scan the room, not looking for anyone in particular, when I spot Emilio walking toward Roman with a concerned frown etched into his face. He says something in Roman's ear before pointing across the room. Roman's head jerks in that direction and I follow his gaze to find a petite blond beside Hunt. I can't see her face with her back toward me, but I'll assume she's his date given the way he hovers beside her, his eyes possessive on her face.

Flicking my attention between them and the guys, my mind spins, trying to uncover the problem. Emilio is worked up, not bothering to be discreet any longer as he says something to Roman, waving his hands in the air. Alejandra stands beside them with a furrow between her brows. Seeing me looking, she forces out a smile before nudging Roman with her elbow to get his attention.

He turns to her and she jerks her head at me. Letting me know that whatever the problem is, it involves me. When Roman looks my way, a flash of something darkens his gaze. He says something else that I can't hear.

Frustration courses through me and I turn back to Hunt, only this time, I can make out his date's profile. With her hair pulled away from her face in a ballerina's knot, I'm able to see her heart-shaped face, full lips, and delicate nose.

What. The. Fuck?

My ears ring, my feet moving before I've even processed what I'm going to do next. The fingers on my arm tighten, keeping me in place.

I turn my dark glare to my date, wordlessly ordering her to let go.

"What do you think you're doing?" she hisses between her teeth, nails digging into my arm as she throws a comment over her shoulder and steers me away. "You can't storm over there." Strain brackets her mouth as she maintains her forced smile. "You'll cause a scene."

I don't care. "Let go," I growl, voice pitched low, but there's no mistaking my vicious intent. I could break her hold easily enough. This is the only warning she'll get from me.

Her lips thin and she relaxes her grip. "You're making a mistake."

Her hand falls away with my next step. "I'm sorry," I tell her, meaning it.

She huffs out an exasperated breath. "It's fine. I'll keep your mother busy as long as I can. Go get her."

On the drive over, Tamara hammered me with questions about Kasey, and for some unknown reason, I answered them. She knows the gist of what's going on between us. I told her Kasey was my girl. The whole point in telling her was so she understood why I needed to bring our fake relationship to a close. It didn't feel right leaving with Tamara. There was hurt in Kasey's eyes. A look of betrayal.

It didn't sit right with me.

Tamara called me an idiot in the car for not telling Kasey about the dinner ahead of time, but I've been so fucking busy, and it never dawned on me that Kasey was in the dark about things. The guys know shit with Tamara is fake, and I assumed someone would have said something. That Kasey knew.

When she fled down the hallway, I told myself I'd explain everything to her as soon as the dinner ended. What if it's too late?

Fuck. Tamara was right. I should have found the time to tell her.

It's Deacon who spots me first, giving me an arrogant smirk. Teammate or not, I will pummel his face into the ground if he touches her.

"What's up, *bro*?" The way he emphasizes the word bro is mocking.

I ignore him and grab Kasey by the arm, spinning her around to face me.

"What are you doing?" she grits through her teeth.

Roman, Allie, and Emilio step up beside me, forming a half circle around us. They must have headed this way when I did.

"Everything good?" Roman asks.

"Yeah." Deacon grabs Kasey by the elbow and draws her back to him.

Fury roars through my bloodstream and my fingers dig into the hold I have on her other arm, refusing to let go.

Kasey winces and I bite out a curse before releasing her.

"Can I talk to you?" It takes everything in me to ask, knowing now isn't the time to approach her with any demands.

"I'm busy." I don't miss the way she worries her bottom lip as she says, "You should go back to your date."

Willing myself not to cause a scene, I step closer until she's trapped between Deacon and I. Dipping my voice low, I lean in close to whisper into her ear, not giving a shit if he hears me. "What the fuck are you doing here with him?"

It's Deacon who answers. "I invited her. Does that bother you?" He glances around before tilting his head in the direction I left Tamara. "Why don't you spend the evening with your date so I can enjoy the evening with mine."

Over my dead body.

My hand curls into a fist and I glower at him before looking down at Kasey and dismissing him entirely.

"I told you I'd only be here for a few hours."

Bright blue eyes meet mine and she lifts one shoulder in a half-hearted shrug. "Cool. I'll see you around."

Is she for real? "Kasey—"

"Dominique, what is going on over here?" My mother's voice cuts through the air. Shit. Closing my eyes, I take a deep breath before forcing myself to turn and face her.

"Nothing is going on," I tell her. "Just talking with friends."

Deacon snorts behind me, but I ignore it.

My mother's attention flicks over Roman, Emilio, Allie, and Deacon in disinterest, but when she cranes her neck to see Kasey, her gaze lingers. Eyes narrowed, she tries to get a better look at my girl.

"Friends?" There's a bite in her voice. "What sort of friend is she?" She gives me an expectant look and I move to my right, exposing Kasey to her gaze. If I didn't, she'd just walk around me.

Kasey, for what it's worth, offers my mother a polite smile and introduces herself, ignoring the tension that hangs like a heavy curtain in the room.

"I'm Kasey. It's nice to meet you." She holds out her hand and my mother eyes it like you would a bug under a microscope, making it clear she has no intention of shaking it.

Kasey drops her arm to her side, keeping her smile in place, but the light in her eyes dims.

Deacon takes a step closer to her, running his hand up and down her back to comfort her. Kasey swallows hard and leans into his touch.

Fucking hell.

"Did you need something?" My tone is sharp, bordering on disrespectful, but she made Kasey feel like shit for no fucking reason than because she could.

My family would never approve of Kasey, but after meeting with Andres DeAnde I realized when it comes to my parents' approval, I don't fucking care.

Why should their opinions matter when they've never cared about mine? My whole life they've tried to mold me into their perfect image, and in a way, I've accepted it.

Not anymore.

"Yes. Your father and I wanted to discuss your engagement—
"

Kasey stiffens, blood draining from her face.

"—to Tamara."

"There is no engagement," I grind out.

I want to turn to Kasey and tell her there is no engagement. That this is just my mother's bullshit delusion, but my mother saw Kasey's reaction, and like the viper she is, she moves in to strike.

"Sweetheart, your father and I know you want to wait until graduation—"

Kasey sucks in a ragged breath as Deacon says, "Come on."

I don't need to look to know he's pulling Kasey away.

"Wait." I reach for her, my fingers brushing the bare skin on her arm.

"Dominique—"

"Mother. Stop!" I snap, raising my voice. I won't let her ruin this for me. I am done letting my parents dictate my life.

My mother rears back. "Young man, don't you—"

I cut her off. "Tamara and I are friends. There is no engagement and there never will be. Get the idea out of your head because hell will freeze over before it ever happens."

My friends each give me a nod of approval, but if they think my mother will give up that easily, they're in for a surprise. Sheridan Price doesn't give up when she doesn't get her way. She buckles down for the fight.

"Don't be silly. Your father and I have it all planned out." She laughs, but the sound is brittle. "It'll be in the spring. Or maybe summer. There will—"

"Is everything okay?" Tamara steps up beside my mother, and Sheridan Price uses the opportunity to take another shot.

"Everything is fine dear, we were discussing your impending engagement—" She gives Tamara an expectant look and Tamara turns wide eyes toward me. Her gaze begs to know how she's supposed to respond.

I shake my head, giving her a look she thankfully understands. With a nod, she gives me the final push I need to blow up the carefully planned life I've led up to this moment. It's been a long time coming.

"There is *no* engagement. Get that through your head." I enunciate each word, saying it loud enough that a hush falls over the room and the people closest to us turn their heads and stare.

My mother cringes at the unwanted attention. "You are causing a scene," she hisses.

"I don't care." Reaching out, I grab Kasey's hand and tug her into my side. "Mother, this is Kasey. The woman I'm seeing." I dip my head to Tamara. "T's been nice enough to act as a stand-in for your benefit, but there's never been anything going on between us. It's always been a show."

Kasey's mouth opens and closes, but nothing comes out. That's okay. I have plenty to say for the both of us.

My mother sputters. "I will not allow you to—"

"And you'll see the press release soon enough, but I'm dropping out of college."

She staggers on her feet, hand clutched to her chest like my words pain her. It's all an act.

"I accepted an offer to play for the Royals."

That, more than anything else I've said, twists her face with anger. "You will do no such thing."

My sister chooses that moment to join the conversation. With a hand on our mother's arm, she tries to defuse the situation. "Mom, breathe. Why don't I drive you home? You can call Dominique tomorrow, or maybe in a few days after you've had some time to process things."

Her nostrils flare.

Monique tries again. "Mom—?"

"You're Dom's sister?" Deacon asks, stepping up beside me. It's then that I notice Kasey's wide, worried eyes. *It's okay, baby girl. We'll leave in a few minutes.*

Monique doesn't let his interruption distract her. "Yes. I'm Monique." She tugs on our mother, who's still not moving. "You are?"

Deacon blinks hard and glares at me. "You have a sister!"

I do. So what?

"Fuck," he curses, running his hand over his hair. "You knew about her?" His question is directed at Kasey. Her head dips into a barely perceptible nod. What am I missing here? His light eyes slice through me like I purposefully withheld my sister's existence from him.

"Hey, man," Emilio draws Deacon's attention. "Let's all go our separate ways. Cool off for a bit."

A vein pulses in Deacon's neck and he shakes his head before looking at Kasey again. She gives him a look of encouragement, but I don't know what for.

Sucking on his teeth, he comes to some sort of decision and looks at Monique once more. Holding out his hand, he says four words I never thought I would hear. "I'm your half brother."

She stares at him unblinkingly before turning to me with wide eyes. "Our what?"

"The fuck?"

Kasey tugs on my arm and I look down to see her mouth the words, "It's true."

"He's my brother?"

She nods.

"And you knew?" She knew and she didn't tell me.

"I asked her not to tell you," Deacon says.

"Why?"

He barks out a laugh. "Are you kidding? Dom, you hate me."

"You're a dick," I tell him.

"So are you." He might have a point.

"How are you our brother?" Monique asks, but she doesn't look bothered by the idea. If anything, she's excited.

"Affair. Your dad and my mom. Things didn't work out." He laughs, but there's no humor in his voice.

My mother's face is ashen, but there's no surprise in her gaze.

"You knew?" I ask.

She ignores the question. "Come on, dear." She pulls on Monique's arm, but this time, my sister isn't so willing to leave.

'Wait. So you're—"

"That's enough of that," my mother snaps. "He is not your brother. He is the byproduct of a mistake."

I wince, and Monique's eyes widen to the size of saucers before she gathers her composure and in an imitation of my mother says, "I'll see you back out the house. You can leave."

With a huff, my mother surprises me and does exactly that.

"Do you want to maybe ..." Monique chews on her lip. "Grab a cup of coffee? I'm only in town for the night and will fly out tomorrow morning but—" Her eyes flick to mine, a silent request, but I can't. I need to fix things with Kasey.

"You two go. We can talk later."

Monique nods. "So, umm. Is that okay?" she asks Deacon.

His smile is wide when he says, "Yeah. I'd like that."

Leaving them to it, I steer Kasey forward with my hand on the small of her back, leading her toward the main doors. She seems stunned for the first few seconds, following my lead without protest, but as soon as we're outside and the evening air hits us, she whirls away from me.

"What was that?" She wraps her arms around herself, goosebumps breaking out across her pale skin.

Peeling off of my jacket, I drape it around her shoulders to keep her warm. She tries to shrug out of it, but I pull on the lapels, tugging her closer and wrapping the jacket more firmly around her.

"Which part?" A lot happened in such a short amount of time.

I nudge her into motion, leading her to my Escalade. The sooner we're away from here, the better.

The drive back to my place is filled with an uncomfortable silence. More than once, I part my lips, intent on breaking it. But what do I say?

I claimed her in front of everyone and announced our relationship without knowing what we are. Only that I'm unwilling to give her up. I still need to clear the air on the stuff about Tamara. Make sure Kasey understands there was never anyone else. I fucked up. I'll own that.

And now I have a half brother I didn't know about. One that she did. *Fuck.* She should have told me. I don't know how to feel about the fact that she didn't. How long has she known?

We both fucked up, and yeah, maybe I'm more than a little pissed. But more than that, I'm fucking relieved. I don't have to lie anymore. To play the twisted game of *Life* my parents have set out for me. I accepted DeAnde's offer before leaving the restaurant, and now my mother knows it. Soon enough, she'll inform my father, but it won't make a difference.

I'm free.

TWENTY-ONE
KASEY

"Y ou going to talk to me, baby girl?" Dominique asks as
soon as we get to his place.

No.

Jumping out of the car, I head for the sidewalk. My place is
only a few blocks away.

With his hands around my waist, Dominique draws me close,
his breath warm against my ear. "Where do you think you're
going?"

"Home."

He shakes his head and turns me to face him.

"You're coming inside with me." It's not a question.

"Aaron—"

"Isn't here." He points toward the empty driveway.
"Come on."

Reluctantly, I let him drag me inside while nervous energy skitters beneath my skin. The back of my neck burns and I tug Dom's jacket off, suddenly overheated.

Leaving him by the door, I walk over to the kitchen and pour myself a glass of water.

Dominique follows me. After downing half of the glass, he takes it from my fingers and sets it aside on the counter. I avoid his eyes as Dominique looks down at me before tipping my chin up with his knuckles, forcing me to meet his gaze.

"You're acting weird."

"No, I am not." His hand spreads to cup my cheek and I jerk back before moving around him. I can't think when he touches me, and there is a lot I need to think about.

"Yes, you are."

"Am not."

"Are too."

"Am not."

"Are too."

God, he is infuriating. "Will you let this go? I need"—I suck in a shuddering breath—"space."

His jaw flexes as he clips out one word. "Space?"

"Yes."

Dominique shakes his head and prowls after me. "No can do, baby girl." His words are rough as he stalks me like a hunter who's marked me as his prey. "We're getting our shit figured out right here. Right now."

I shake my head in denial and gauge how long it will take me to reach the front door. He must see my intentions in my gaze because a growl vibrates deep in the base of his throat.

"Kasey—" he warns.

No. Nope. No. I shove past him and bolt for the door.

"Kasey!" he shouts after me, hot on my heels. He tackles me to the floor, shifting our positions at the last second so I land on top of him with his arms banded around my waist.

"Will you just talk to me?"

I shake my head, letting my blond curls cover my face as I fight against his hold, but it's no use.

With a snarl, he grabs my throat and jerks me closer before slamming his lips against mine.

I keep my lips tight at first, but he traces his tongue over the seam of my mouth, demanding entry until my lips part on a gasp. He answers my submission with a groan.

Flipping our positions, he rolls me to my back and presses me into the carpet while his hands wander over my body, finding the slit of my dress and exposing my thigh.

"Will you stop fighting me now?" he grumbles and nips at my lower lip.

"Never," I tell him.

"Have it your way." He climbs to his feet and I try to ignore my disappointment at his easy dismissal. Helping me to my feet, I assume this is where we part ways, but instead of letting go, Dominique throws me over his shoulder.

"Hey!" I squirm in his hold. "Put me down."

One arm wraps around my thighs, keeping me in place on his shoulder while his other hand grabs my ass.

"You don't want to talk." His voice is thick.

Smack.

"We won't talk."

I jerk in his arms and my pussy clenches, liquid heat spilling between my thighs.

"But remember, baby girl. We could have done this the easy way."

"We could?" My chest heaves and the next thing I know, he's kicking the door to his room closed behind him and throwing me across the bed.

I land on my back, bouncing once before he's on top of me.

"Yeah. We could. But now, we're going to do things my way."

DOMINIQUE'S WAY involves multiple orgasms until I can't breathe, let alone speak. Not that I wanted to do any talking.

He fucks me all night and early into the morning, our bodies saying everything our mouths are unwilling to say.

I need this. Need him. But no longer in the same way. And while recent revelations only confirm what I already knew, that this is temporary, I allow myself one last indulgence.

One night to relish the press of his skin against mine. To remember the look on his face and the sound of his groan when he sinks his length inside of me.

I can't get enough.

We sleep in small intervals after finding our release with one another, pausing to catch our breath and close our eyes. Sometimes it's only for a handful of minutes, others it's an hour. But it's never long before one of us glides across the other's body and we're back at it again.

I'm used to Dominique's rough brand of pleasure. To being dominated by him between the sheets. And the first two times he takes me is like that. But everything is... I shiver thinking about it.

Dominique slowed our kisses and gentled his touch before settling me low on his hips and lying back on his pillow, watching as I sank down onto his length.

His expression was open, emotions unmasked. I don't know if he realized the finality of what we were doing. If he acknowledged the way I was saying goodbye.

He falls asleep around four in the morning, and I wait ten minutes, assuring myself he won't wake up for a while now before slipping free from his arms to retrieve my dress from where we discarded it earlier.

Slipping into the material, I give his naked, sleeping form one last look before forcing my feet to move. This is goodbye. Not forever. We'll see each other again. But at the McIntire dinner, he said he'd accepted an offer from the Richland Royals. And while I know now that there was nothing for me to worry about with Tamara, I also realize I can't put myself through that again.

With my earlier hurt still fresh in my mind, I walk out of his house. Every step I take away from him makes the hole in my heart tear more, but I don't stop.

Head held high, I try to find comfort in the fact that this time, I'm the one walking away.

I wake to find the space beside me empty and the sheets already cold. Looking around the room, I don't spot Kasey or any sign of her having been here last night. That's okay. I'll track her down later. Remind her of that fact she can't keep running away. Sooner or later we're going to talk, and if I have it my way, it'll be the next time I see her.

Throwing on a pair of shorts, I go straight to the kitchen to turn on the coffee pot but find that it's already on. Frowning, I go to the living room and look out the window. Aaron's Subaru is still gone from our driveway.

Hmm... Maybe one of us left it on the day before? Turning back, I come to a hard stop when my gaze lands on a shirtless Aaron seated on one of the barstools. Rubbing the sleep from my eyes, I take him in again. Still there. Not hallucinating.

"When did you get in?" I ask, eyeing him warily as I pour myself a cup of coffee. Is that why Kasey bolted this morning? Did she hear him when he got in?

"Before you got home and banged my baby sister all night."

Fuck. My stomach drops.

I open my mouth. Close it. Consider my words. *Fuck.*

Aaron moves around me toward the cupboard and refills his coffee mug. "Take your time," he says, and walks back to his seat. "I can wait."

I scrub my hand over my face. None of the explanations I have sound good enough. "Don't know what to say to that," I admit with a grimace. This is what I'd been trying to avoid.

He works his jaw and levels me with a knowing look before leaning back on the counter. He blows over his coffee before taking a sip, his attention never leaving my face.

"How long?"

I consider lying, but I get the feeling he either knows, or has a solid suspicion for when shit with Kasey and I started. Lying to him now will only make things worse.

"Since your mom passed away."

He nods. I'm having a hard time reading him. I expected him to blow up. Shout. Or maybe take a swing at me. What I did not expect is this detached inquisition.

"So instead of looking out for my little sister, like you promised to—" he holds a hand up, stopping me from defending myself, not that I have much of a leg to stand on here, "you take advantage of her when she's grieving and think to yourself, *hey, now sounds like a great time to get my dick wet.*"

"It wasn't like that."

His expression is mocking. "No? Then what the fuck is it like, Dom? Because from where I'm sitting, you took advantage of the most important person in my life. The person I'm supposed to protect from assholes like you." He shakes his head, his lip curling in disgust. "I trusted you, man."

"I know. I didn't mean for shit to happen the way it did, but—"

"But what?" he demands. "What happens now, Dom? Is it serious? Are you dating my sister now?" He doesn't give me the chance to answer. "Of course not. Dominique Price doesn't commit. He doesn't do relationships. You fuck and then you move on. Just this time, you made my sister one of your whores."

"Don't call her that." There's a warning in my voice. I don't care if he's pissed with me. If he calls her a whore again, I'm knocking his lights out.

His jaw tightens. "Tell me I'm wrong, then."

"You are."

He sets his cup down and shoves away from the counter, getting into my face. "Yeah? Then what is it, huh? Explain it to me."

I shove him away from me, but he surges forward, eliminating the distance between us and baring his teeth in my face.

"It's complicated," I growl.

His smile is bitter. "I'm sure it is. Because Dominique Price can't be in a relationship with a white girl, right? Dominique Price, who has his whole fucking life planned out for him, has to marry a sophisticated black woman. One with the right background who comes from the right family. The Prices are prestigious. They hold themselves to higher standards." He stabs his finger into my chest. "You forget, I know everything about you. Your parents agree to look the other way while you lower yourself to play ball in college because they know when the time comes, you'll fall in line. So you know you can't have her, but you fucked around with her anyway."

He steps back, expression hard and filled with disgust. "I've told you since high school to stay the hell away from her. You swore you wouldn't go there."

"I know."

"You lied."

"I know. But—"

"There is no *but*, man. Don't you get that? She's had a thing for you since fucking high school, so whatever you think you're doing, however casual you think it is, it's not the same for her."

"She didn't like me in high school," I retort, though it's a moot point. I'm keeping her now.

"Yeah, man. She did. And I thought you were decent enough to stay the fuck away because you knew—" He slices me open with his glare. "You knew nothing could come of it. She doesn't have a chance with you. Not a real one."

He turns his back to me, bracing his hands on the counter. His shoulders are stiff, arms flexing as he struggles to rein himself in. To be honest, I'm surprised he bothers. If I were him, I'd have punched myself in the face by now.

"I think I love her, man." I haven't said the words out loud before, but they're true. Last night made me realize a lot of things. Not only am I falling for her, but I want a life with her. I want forever.

"Does it even fucking matter?" he asks, not looking at me.

"Yeah. It does." He still doesn't turn around, but that's okay. He'll come around. Right now he's pissed because he thinks I'm doing wrong by her. He doesn't know everything.

"I told my mom Tamara and I have never been anything more than friends."

He barks out a laugh. "Bet that went well."

"I also told her I'm with your sister."

His head snaps toward me. "You did what?" He twists back around to face me. "Don't fuck with me right now."

"I'm not. I meant what I said. I think I'm in love with her, man. I didn't plan any of this. It's been messy and complicated from the beginning, and we've had more than our fair share of ups and downs, but," I shrug, "I want her."

"For now?"

I shake my head. "Nah. Forever."

"You're serious."

"I am."

He swallows hard. "So what's your plan?"

And that's the million dollar question. "Don't know. Guess I figure out if she wants a forever with me, too. If she doesn't—" I shrug and finish the thought in my head. I won't accept that shit. I'll tie her infuriating ass to my bed and fuck her until the lust in her eyes turns into love if I have to. I'm not giving the girl up. No fucking way.

"I'm tempted to kick your ass for going behind my back and sleeping with my sister. That's messed up."

"I'll give you a free shot." Tapping the edge of my jaw, I wait to see if he'll take me up on the offer.

He doesn't.

"Nah," he says. "If you're serious about trying to lock down my sister, Kasey's going to fuck you up way worse than I ever could."

"She already has, man. She already has."

WITH THE AARON crisis set aside, I move on to tracking Kasey down, but she doesn't answer her phone and she isn't returning my calls. After taking a shower and grabbing something to eat, I swing by the Kappa Mu house to catch her there. I don't want there to be any more questions between us. We're going to figure things out.

But when I pull up into the small lot where her car is supposed to be, I find her parking space empty and don't bother going inside.

News broke this morning that I'm being taken before the draft to join the Richland Royals, and my phone has been ringing nonstop since, but none of the numbers are Kasey's.

My father calls four times, but I ignore each one. I know what he wants, and he won't get it from me. I'm done doing what he wants.

Roman's name flashes on my screen and I look down, not seeing any message, but instead there is an attachment. Clicking on the thumbnail, a photograph someone snapped of me and Kasey at the McIntire dinner pops up on my screen, followed by a text.

Roman: This is circulating around. Handle it.

I SIGH.

Me: Already on it.

IT WAS SHARED in the news, too. Broadcasters speculate Kasey and I are in a romantic relationship and several have left me messages asking for a comment.

I wanted to talk to Kasey about everything first, but I'm running short on time, and I need these vultures off my back. When the next call comes in with a number I don't recognize, I take a leap and go for broke. There's that saying that actions speak louder than words. Maybe if I combine the two, things with Kasey will lean more in my favor.

"Dominique, do you have any comment regarding rumors of your relationship with Suncrest U freshman, Kasey Henderson?" a chirpy reporter asks before I even get the chance to say hello.

"Yeah, she's my girl," I grunt, straight to the point.

"Oooh. Tell me more."

"What do you want to know?" I keep the call short, confirming we're in a relationship and have been since high school. It's not a complete lie. We've had this strange back and forth since then, anyway.

Ending the call, I flip my phone to silent and park my car on campus. I know I'm not the only one being hammered with questions like this, and if she's not home, the only other place she can be while she hides from me and the rest of the world is here.

You can run, baby girl. But you can't hide. Not forever.

TWENTY-THREE
KASEY

I t's after five when he finds me. I've kept myself holed up in the school's library most of the day. I saw the picture of myself in the news this morning and knew things were going to turn into a shit show.

"Hey, baby girl. What are you working on?" His voice is casual as he walks over to the table where I sit, my books and notes strewn all over.

"Hey." I turn back to my notes and ignore the way my heart is now racing inside my chest.

A wooden chair scrapes across the floor when he grabs one from another table and pulls it over to where I'm at. "Studying?"

"Mm hmm." *So you should leave me alone and let me finish.*

But of course, he's not interested in doing that.

"We need to talk."

A lump of dread clogs my throat, and I keep my gaze locked on my papers as I scribble out random words on my notes. "About?"

"Us."

My hand freezes from writing, and I set my pen down before flicking my gaze up. "There isn't an us," I shrug. "So we have nothing to talk about."

"Don't do that," he growls. "Don't run away."

Scratching my forehead, I sigh. "I'm not running, Dom." This is self-preservation."Why are you pushing this?" We both know the score. Let's call this what it is and walk away before any more damage is done. I can't take it.

"Because you're hiding—"

"I'm not. I'm right here in the library where anyone can see me. This isn't hiding, Dominique. It's called doing homework. Something you don't have to worry about because you're dropping out to play football."

His glare burrows into me. "Is that a problem?" he asks. "Me not finishing my degree?"

What? No! "I don't care if you get a degree or not. It makes no difference to me." Except I'll be here, and he won't be. He'll be playing football. Traveling. Seeing the world and meeting a bunch of new people.

"Talk to me, Kasey. Are you still upset because of Tamara?" He releases a harsh breath. "I fucked up," he begins, and the fact I think he's going to apologize is the only reason I keep my mouth closed and listen. Dominique Price never says he's sorry. "I thought you knew about our arrangement. Figured one of the guys, or maybe Aaron, would have told you."

"They didn't."

His shoulders drop. "I know. I'm sorry."

Hearing him apologize doesn't feel as great as I thought it would. "Okay," I tell him and it is. I won't hold the Tamara stuff against him. What would be the point? It doesn't change anything.

"What is it then? What did I do?"

I shake my head, a small smile on my face. "Nothing, Dom. You did nothing."

He curses. "Things were good last night."

My cheeks heat. "They were."

"But they're not now?"

I shake my head. "Things are fine now. Just... different."

"Different how?"

I collect my things and shove them into my bag. "You're going to play for the Royals,"

"I thought you'd be happy for me." He sounds genuinely confused, which makes this harder.

"I am. You deserve it. But—"

Dominique gets out of his chair and crouches down beside me. He cups my face in his hands, his gaze boring into mine with an intense look tinged with fear. It steals my breath away.

"But what?"

Closing my eyes, I lean into his touch before saying, "But the Royals are in Richland, which means you're moving."

His brows furrow as he takes in my words before realization hits. "Come with me."

I huff out a breath. "Why?" I ask. "What reason do I have for uprooting my entire life for you?"

"Because..."

His mouth twists into a grimace. *Like I thought.* Because what?

"You can't pretend you expected a different outcome. We both knew the score. This was always going to be temporary."

His jaw flexes and his eyes flash with anger. "Bullshit," he snarls.

"We're not together, Dom. We never have been."

"We could be," he says, but it's not a question. He isn't asking me to be his girlfriend. He's not asking me to be anything, yet he expects me to drop my life and chase after him so I can, what, continue being his fuck buddy? No. I won't do that to myself.

"I deserve better," I tell him, pulling away.

Sitting back on his heels, he regards me. "I want a chance."

I almost laugh. "A chance at what, exactly?"

"The real deal," he says. "You and me."

"You're leaving," I remind him.

"So?"

"I won't go with you."

His eyes shutter.

"Even if I wanted to," I say, trying to soften the blow, "I can't. I have to graduate. That has to come first." I don't have the option of transferring schools. Not until I have my diploma.

"And then?" He's being serious. This is insane.

"I don't know," I whisper honestly. I didn't expect him to show up like this and say he wanted to be with me. I thought he wanted to clear the air to keep access to my pussy, not jump into a relationship.

This is getting complicated. Heavy.

"Will you give things between us a try?" he asks, his expression pensive.

"It won't work."

"It could." He sounds sure but I'm not.

"You're going to be in a new town. You'll meet other people. Other women—"

"Don't delude yourself, Kasey. There won't be any other women." His thumb traces my bottom lip before he leans forward to kiss me. "It was always going to be the two of us in the end, baby girl. This—" He threads his fingers through my hair and kisses deeper, stealing the breath from my lungs. "Us." Another kiss. His tongue traces the seam of my lips. "It was inevitable"

Sucking in a breath at his declaration, I confess the one thing I'm terrified of most. He's putting his cards out there. This is my way of showing mine.

"You could hurt me." It pains me to admit that. To show him my vulnerable parts and confess he has that much power over me.

Dominique leans back to look me in the eyes, thumbs stroking across my cheeks. "Trust me, Kasey. I won't."

I want to trust him. I really do. But there's a battle going on inside of me and I have no idea how this will play out. The odds are already stacked against us. And after everything we've been through, can long distance even work?

"Promise me." They're only words, but if I'm going to consider this, I need to hear them.

His eyes are reverent as he holds my gaze. "I won't hurt you, baby girl. I swear."

Dom and Kasey aren't finished yet.
Keep an eye out for the third and final book in the Dom &
Kasey trilogy. No pre-order yet but make sure you're in my
reader group since I'll be sharing details soon.

If you haven't guessed it already, A LOT of things are going
to happen in Richland. To make sure you're up to date, check
out The Savage. This is Gabriel & Cecilia's Story—you met
Gabe at the end of Wicked Devil—and pre-order Vicious
Little Liar where you'll see Andres DeAnde brought to his
knees by a rivals daughter in this Romeo & Juliette retelling
without the tragic ending.

To get a head start, keep scrolling for the first three chapters
of The Savage, available now and in kindle unlimited.

Cecilia - 3 months earlier

I WAKE TO A DRY MOUTH, a sluggish brain, and
a pounding headache. God, how much did I have to drink last
night? Just turning to the side, my face still mashed against
the pillow, sends a spear of agony stabbing into my skull.

I let out a pain filled groan and a wave of nausea slams into
me. Fuck. I think I'm going to be sick. Sightlessly, I reach out
to get my bearings and fumble to get myself in a seated
position so I can make a run for the bathroom. Or walk. I

swallow the lump in my throat. Right now, I'll settle for a crawl.

My fingers cling to the sheets beneath me and I shove up.

Wait a minute. I clench and unclench the material beneath my hands. That's not right. It's thick. Flannel. But that can't be right. My sheets are cotton. Light and thin because I hate waking up in the middle of the night overheated.

This isn't my bed.

Forcing my sticky eyelids open, I push the long tangled strands of my dark brown hair out of my face and take in my surroundings. Blinking hard against the hazy light that filters in through the window, I stare down at the very blue fabric beneath me. Definitely not mine.

Where the hell am I?

I scan the room. It's decidedly a boy's. Posters of half-naked girls leaning against muscle cars decorate the walls, intermixed with athletic trophies and sports paraphernalia.

Classy.

Swinging my legs over the side of the bed, I scoot to the end, but have to pause when the room spins and everything along the edges of my vision blurs.

I've been hungover before, but never like this, where my entire body aches and I can't remember why I'm in someone else's bed. Slowly, so as not to black out, I glance over my shoulder and exhale a breath of relief. Not my bed, but whoever's it is, they're thankfully not in it with me. That's something, at least.

I turn back around with a sigh of relief but it's short lived when I look down and notice the state of my dress. It's torn down the front, my chest spilling out of the ruined satin and lace. I clutch at the material, bringing it together, but it's no use.

Something hard pokes me under my arm and I fumble around inside my dress, finding the edges of my bra. Untwisting the damn thing, I bring the front clasp together, satisfied at least that my boobs are no longer on display.

That's when I see the bruises. I haven't let myself think beyond the pounding in my head and the nausea twisting my gut, but now, holding my hands out in front of me, I take in the dark purple smudges that circle both of my wrists and forearms.

What the hell happened to me?

I stare at them in abject horror, rotating my arm to see all the way around. Are those... finger marks? I don't like the scenarios my mind conjures up. The numerous ways I could have gotten bruises like this. None of them are good.

This is the stuff you see in movies. Not real life. Not to someone like me.

I need... I — it hits me and my chest heaves, breath seesawing in and out. This isn't real. It's a dream. A bad, bad dream.

I squeeze my eyes closed and clutch my hands to my chest. I remember going out with Kim and Joelle. The Zeta Pi party. Austin.

Bile climbs up my throat and I cover my mouth with my hand. Thick, oily dread settles into my veins. I really am going to be sick. I stumble to my feet but my legs give out beneath me and I crash to the hardwood floor. My knees smart and tears pool in my eyes, but it's not the pain that causes my emotions to well up inside me.

It's memories of last night assaulting my mind that do that for me.

He... he... I squeeze my eyes closed. No! Tears spill over my cheeks and track down my face. When I open them again, I spot a waste bin beside the bedside table and lunge for it, barely making it before my stomach empties itself.

This isn't happening.

Cool air hits the backs of my thighs, informing me that my chest isn't the only part of me exposed.

I vomit again.

Please be a nightmare. A sick and twisted figment of my imagination. But it isn't, and knowing that has a keening sound slipping past my lips. This is real. It's sick and not okay, but what happened to me, it's real.

My stomach is empty now, but I continue to dry heave. It's like my body revolts against the revelation of what's transpired.

Gut wrenching sobs wrack my body and I try my damndest to muffle them. I don't know if anyone else is here. If Austin is still around.

What will he do if he finds me? I can't wait to find out.

Wiping my mouth with the back of my hand, I begin the frantic search for my shoes. I don't see them anyway, but manage to spot my phone.

On shaking limbs, I force myself to get up and retrieve it. My entire body is sore, like one big bruise has taken up residence on every inch of skin I possess. Grabbing my cell, I swipe my thumb over the screen. Nothing. I do it again.

Dammit. It's dead.

Voices in the hall freeze me where I stand. I strain my ears. More than one and all male by the sounds of it. Every muscle in me locks up.

Footsteps move closer to the door. Shit. My fingers tighten around my phone, clenching it as if it's my last lifeline.

What do I do?

I scan the room, searching for something, anything, I can use as a weapon but there's nothing.

Footsteps pause on the other side of the door. The knob twists. I watch in horror as it turns three quarters of the way before stopping, almost like whoever stands on the other side knows I'm waiting.

On silent hinges, the door swings open to reveal Austin Holt. PacNorth's star soccer player. Head of Zeta Pi fraternity. And the man I know will soon haunt my nightmares.

"You're up." His blue eyes take in my disheveled appearance, and he smirks. "We need to talk."

Gabriel

"MAMÁ? POPS?" I call out, stepping through the door.

No answer, not that it surprises me. I ignore the lack of response and step further into my childhood home. The house is quiet. Still. But I don't let it deter me.

There's this oppressive sense of loss that hangs heavy in the air and settles on my shoulders like a physical weight. One I've learned I cannot escape so long as I am here.

I hate it.

This used to be home. My haven. Now, it's nothing more than the tomb that holds a collection of broken memories. Ones I am desperate to forget.

Being here makes my muscles tighten in anticipation. Like another bomb is about to drop. Only this time, I have some measure of warning. Too bad knowing what's coming doesn't make it hurt any less. If anything, it makes matters worse. They know exactly what they're doing and have made it clear, they don't care.

Pictures line the walls, an eclectic collage my mother put together over the years while I was growing up, but more striking than the images themselves are the gaps interspersed throughout them. The faded shapes where picture frames once stood but have long since been removed.

My fingers trail over one particular gap. My brother's and my first steps. We were just under a year old and stood in our front yard, excited grins on our faces at what we'd just accomplished. Even with it gone, I can see the image in my head as though Mom never took it down.

I drag my hand further along the wall, trailing around the frames that still hold photographs of friends and relatives through the years until I reach the spot in the center that once served as the focal point of our family gallery. It held my parents' wedding photo but now it's empty, the paint darker here having been protected from the sun. I shake my head. It's been like this for months, but I still can't get used to it. It's like the soul of the house died. Right along with any love our family had for one another.

There are more empty spots than there are filled. Anything with Carlos was removed after his death. Family portraits. His school pictures. Following that, Mom took down pictures of me. Seeing my face became too much for her. A constant reminder of the son she lost. I used to wish we didn't share a face. That he'd never been my twin.

Now, I just don't care.

She should have taken all the photographs down. It'd look less... I don't know, depressing, maybe, if she had.

I drop my helmet on the entryway table, ready to get this over with, and cut through the foyer on my way to the kitchen. Despite not getting an answer when I first arrived, I know my parents are home. They're the ones who scheduled this bullshit meeting today, after all.

Dad's leaning against the kitchen counter when I step into the room, a glass of amber liquid in his hand. No surprise there. The man hasn't been sober in months.

Mom sits at the dining room table, claiming the seat furthest from him with a glass of wine in front of her. Wonderful.

They knew their son was showing up and both decided alcohol was the best way to deal with it.

Neither of them looks at the other and only Dad bothers to acknowledge me, offering a small nod of his head before he indicates the thick envelope resting atop the kitchen island, my name written in thick black marker across the top of it.

Tension sits heavily in the room. I've only just walked in and already it threatens to suffocate me. How long have they been sitting here like this?

"This everything?" The sooner we get this over with, the sooner I can leave.

Mom doesn't look at me, but she does take a heavy drink from her wine glass. Why is she even here? She hasn't spoken to me in months. Neither of them has. I'm surprised they didn't ask me to mail in the papers and save everyone the trouble of being here right now.

"It is," my dad says. "We just need your signature and then we..." he trails off, but I don't need him to finish. Like the two of them, I'm aware of why we're here.

Swallowing past the lump in my throat, I tear open the packet and make quick work signing my name on all the lines their attorney's bothered to highlight in yellow. I don't waste time reading over the documents. This benefits me more than it does them. The sooner we get this over with, the better.

My grandparents set up a trust for my brother and I when we were kids. Nothing crazy, but education has always been a big deal in our family and they wanted to make sure my brother and I had the means to go to college.

If my grandparents were still around, I think they'd be proud to learn I earned a full ride to PacNorth to play soccer. I don't need their money for school. Not that it makes it any less mine.

When Carlos passed away, his portion became mine as well. Something about it being a joint account. With one brother gone, the rest falls to the other.

There are stipulations on the account. Carlos and I both gained access when we turned eighteen, but only for expenses directly related to college and each withdrawal requires my parents' consent. Carlos never had the chance to spend so much as a penny and I've never touched a dime. I never needed to. Since I don't need the money for school, I shouldn't have access to the account until after my twenty-fifth birthday. But that's three years from now and for my parents, it's three years of being tied to me, too many.

They've decided to sign over the account early. A few signatures here and there and I no longer need their consent to access any of it. I'll have more money than I could need as a senior in college, and they'll have no reason to see me again.

For them, it's a win-win.

Sometimes I wish I saw it that way.

Closing the packet, I shove the papers back into the envelope and drop it down on the countertop.

"Anything else?"

Dad shakes his head. I turn to Mom, silently begging her to say something, anything. Fuck, I'd be happy if she'd just acknowledged my fucking existence, but she still won't look at me. She sits there, quietly drinking her wine like she can't be bothered. I shouldn't have expected anything less. Mom checked out of my life years ago. I rub the ache in my chest, hating that after all this time, her indifference still affects me. I don't get it. You'd think after losing one kid, they'd fight harder for the other, but instead, they throw me away. It's hard to believe they ever cared about me at all.

"You know..." I shake my head and suck on my teeth. I should drop it. Let this shit go and move on with my life.

My eyes bore into her. I can't, though. This is fucked up. I don't deserve to be treated like this. No one does.

"It's not my fault we share the same face."

Mom flinches but doesn't turn my way. Her throat bobs as she swallows another mouthful of wine, probably wishing I'd hurry up and leave already, but why should I? It's not my problem, she's uncomfortable. That the very site of me, her own fucking son, makes her ill. How does she think it is for me? Waking up and seeing his face every fucking day?

She'll get what she wants soon enough. Once I walk out that door, she can go back to pretending she never had kids. That I'm not her son. That she didn't abandon me when my world was already falling apart. And that making me sign these papers isn't her way of stabbing the knife already buried deeper into my chest.

"Just like it's not my fault he's gone."

Silence.

"It's not my fault he was selfish. Or that he fucked our family over."

"Gabriel—" My father's voice is soft, pleading with me not to fight this. Not to make a scene.

I turn to look at him. "None of this is my fault!" I remind him. "Yet you two are so fucking intent on punishing me for Carlos's sins, anyway."

He hangs his head but says nothing and I don't bother to stick around. All it does is lead to more disappointment.

Grabbing my helmet from the hall, I slam the door behind me, the sound reverberating against my back. I give my childhood home one last look as I climb on my bike.

Fuck them. I didn't need my brother. I sure as hell don't need them.

Cecilia

In case you were wondering, talk is code word for threaten, blackmail, and basically, go out of your way to ruin my life. I should have seen this coming.

"Hey." I wave.

It's lame, but I'm not sure what else to do here. My heart races in my chest as I look from Austin to the door. "I, uh, actually need to leave. I'm sure Joelle and Kim are worried sick that I never came back to the dorms last night."

He either doesn't hear me or, more accurately, doesn't care. And what he does next drops a ball of dread, like a heavy stone, into the pit of my stomach. Austin smiles. It's charming and attractive. Or it would be on anyone else but him. Not after learning what he's capable of.

He steps further into the room and closes the door behind him, locking me inside.

I swallow hard and try not to panic.

Shaking fingers hold the torn front of my dress together as Austin stands there with that stupid smile on his face. He eyes me up and down, like he's remembering what's hidden beneath my dress.

Bile rises from my stomach, coating the back of my throat. I wrap my arms around myself in a desperate attempt at modesty. Like it changes anything.

"What do you want to talk about?" My grip on my phone tightens. I wish the stupid thing wasn't dead. That I could call for help. Before he came in here, he was talking to somebody in the hall, which means we aren't alone.

If I scream, will anybody come help me? Does anybody even know that I'm still here? I think about it. Seriously think about it, because at this point, what have I got to lose?

Austin doesn't look worried, though. He's confident. Hell, relaxed even.

This is a man without a care in the world. Not about me screaming, at least.

"Did you have fun last night?" he asks, breaking the silence.

"Sure. Loads." Lie. I most definitely did not have fun. Being assaulted is not fun. Being forced — I drop that train of thought. Hold it together, Cecilia. Now is not the time or the place. Right now, you need to get the hell out of here. The rest can wait until you're home. Until you're safe.

I force myself to smile. To relax. "But, like I said, I need to get going."

"I get it." Austin casually leans against the door. "Just want to make sure everyone is on the same page. You know how it is. One small misunderstanding can fuel the rumor mill and all of a sudden, a night of fun turns into a bunch of bullshit in the media. Your dad is up for reelection this year, right?" The way he asks, with that curious glint in his eyes, it sets me immediately on edge.

"Why does that— "

He cuts me off. "My parents contributed. To his campaign, I mean. Did you know that?"

I shake my head, not understanding why any of this is relevant to me. My dad is running for Mayor again. Lots of people contribute to his campaign.

"I don't like to brag..."

I barely manage to contain my snort. He's rich, in the Zeta Pi fraternity, on the PacNorth soccer team, and good looking. His ego is bigger than this bedroom and he's one of those guys that likes hearing the sound of his own voice, so he definitely does, in fact, like to brag.

"But my family is a big deal here in Richland." Good for him. "We own Holt & Associates. The law firm down on Twenty-Second Street."

That rock in the pit of my stomach turns into a boulder, and a barely audible gasp slips past my lips.

He hears it, and his smile grows even wider. Holt & Associates is one of my dad's campaign contributors. But more concerning is the fact that they're one of the best known law firms in the state. Hell, maybe even the country. They like high-profile cases. The controversial ones that get their firm on the news, which means more often than not, they represent problematic people. Criminals. And they do a really good job getting them off clean.

"Recognize the name?" He chuckles. "I thought you might. Last I heard, they're one of Russo's largest donors. Your parents and mine are probably good friends." He winks. "Like the two of us."

Indignation floods through me. Friends? Is he serious right now? We are not friends, and I see what he's doing now. "Fuck you."

His eyes flash in surprise. "Excuse me?"

My cheeks heat and I mash my lips together as I bite back my words, but screw it. Screw him. "I know what you're doing." I'm not stupid. I can read just fine between the lines he's so clearly drawing out for me.

Austin quirks a blond brow. "Do you, now?" His tone is condescending. If I was at all confused before, I'm not now.

Nausea sweeps through me when I nod my head, the motion making the room spin, but I manage to hold myself together. "You..." I swallow past the lump in my throat. "You raped— "

"Woah, woah." He holds both hands up in the air. "See. That's what I'm talking about." He makes a tsking sound and shakes his head. "You and I need to get on the same page here, Cece. That sort of accusation can ruin someone's reputation."

My upper lip curls. "Are you screwing with me?"

His eyes are hooded. "I think we did a good amount of that last night, but if you're looking for round two— "

"This isn't a joke." I swing my arm and hurl my phone at his head with every ounce of strength in me. It narrowly misses him, thudding against the wooden door as he jerks out of the way.

Meanwhile, I crash into the dresser beside me as I lose my footing, but I manage to stay on my feet, barely, nails digging into the dresser top.

I bare my teeth. "I'll die before I let you touch me again," I seethe. "Stay the hell away from me."

Austin looks momentarily at a loss for words as he looks from me to my phone and back again before his expression hardens.

"You're not feeling like yourself," he tells me, bending down to retrieve my phone, "so I'm going to make myself clear. What happened last night was— "

"Rape."

He continues on, ignoring me. "A few friends having a good time. We had some drinks. Things got a little out of control."

I'd shake my head if I wasn't so worried I was going to pass out.

"You... you—" I can barely get the words out, but I force myself to say them. "You held me down. You held my hands behind my back while—"

"While my buddies fucked your face," he finishes with a smirk. "Yeah. I did. And you liked it." The look on his face is one of complete satisfaction. He's proud of himself. He makes me sick.

"No. I didn't!" What the hell is wrong with him? How could he possibly think I enjoyed any part of what he did? "You helped your friends assault me and then you—" My brows pinch together. Parts of last night are still a little hazy.

It was late. I was drunk. I wanted to find Kim and Joelle and leave. I remember being tired and when Austin offered to help me find my friends, I took him up on it.

I thought it was kinda sweet. I didn't know him that well, but Kim's had a secret crush on him since freshman year. Having his help was an easy way to introduce the two of them. Give her an in. I talked her up, even. Told him how great my friends were. How Kim was probably his type, and he seemed interested at the time. But it was all just a game to him.

He checked the yard while I checked downstairs, but no luck. When he suggested we check the bedrooms on the second level, I dismissed the idea. No way would either of them hook up with some random at a party. But Austin thought we should look, anyway.

He led me upstairs. I remember thinking it was weird when he bypassed the first two doors. Like he was heading for a specific room. And looking back, it's clear he was.

There were two guys waiting inside, and when I apologized for disturbing them and turned around to leave, Austin blocked my escape. He used his size to press me further into the room, forcing me to stumble back before closing and locking the door behind him.

He planned it. All of it.

"You had it all worked out," I whisper to myself. "The room. The drugs." He drugged me. I remember that now. That must be why my head is so foggy. After he helped his friends, he forced his fingers into my mouth and rubbed something on my gums. A powder of some sort. It tasted awful, but after that, everything starts to fade.

"What was it?" I ask.

"What was what?"

"The drug. Whatever it was you made me take."

He doesn't even bother to deny it. "Ketamine. And don't give me that look. It helped, didn't it? You were more relaxed."

My hands curl into fists. "I didn't want to relax!" I scream. "I wanted to leave. I wanted to get the hell away from you."

He takes a menacing step toward me. "You got what you wanted last night, Cece. Stop deluding yourself. You came to a party dressed like that." He points to my dress. "What did you think was going to happen?"

My mouth hangs open. "No girl wants what you did," I tell him. "Wearing a dress and going to a party isn't asking anyone for what you did."

He snorts. "Stop making this bigger than it needs to be. You gave some good head and got laid. Get that stick out of your ass and move on."

Laid. My mind clings to that word. There were three of him. Did they all—did anyone else —

"Did all three of you rape me?" I can't believe I'm asking him, but I have to know. The last thing I remember after being drugged is Austin laying me on the bed. His hands groping my body. His fingers between my thighs and him climbing on top of me. But after that... nothing.

He glowers at me in silence.

"Answer me," I beg. "Please."

He huffs out a breath and rolls his eyes. "Benson and Chambers fucked your mouth. Only I fucked your cunt. Happy? Can we move this show along now?" He glances at the watch on his wrist. "I have practice to get to."

The way he's so blasé about everything baffles me. He admits to drugging me. To raping me. And yet, he's more worried about getting to practice on time.

"You're not going to get away with this."

He sighs. "Yes, I am. The sooner you realize that, the easier things will get for you."

The horrible thing is, he believes the words coming out of his mouth.

"I'm trying to help you, Cece. Get the two of us on the same page. The right page."

"Don't call me that."

Austin rolls his eyes again. "If you walk out of here and make up stories, it isn't going to end well. Not for you. Be smart."

"Get out."

"Cece—"

"Out!"

He sighs. "Look at the video I texted you." He places my phone on the nearby desk. "I'll send it to your email in case this little outburst of yours broke your cell. Make sure to watch it. You'll reconsider things after you do."

GRAB THE SAVAGE, available now and in kindle unlimited to read more.

I KNOW WHAT YOU'RE THINKING.

What the hell?

Am I right?

Cruel Promise was intended to be the conclusion to Dominique and Kasey's story but I couldn't leave things up in the air with these two.

There are too many questions even I don't have answers to yet and the only way we'll get them, is for me to write a third book.

Will their relationship end before it even has a chance to begin, because Dominique finally has a shot at playing professional football?

And what about Deacon?

Now that Dominique's learned the truth, will he want a relationship with his new found brother?

Will Kasey get caught up with school and earn her diploma in time?

There is so much left to uncover. I hope you'll stick around because Cruel Deliverance and Angry Devil (Aaron's book) are coming up next!

Special thanks to Lisa and Jess for helping me polish Cruel Promise to a shine. You ladies saved my bacon there at the end.

To Jackie, the most amazing assistant in the world, I would be drowning with out you.

To all of the amazing bloggers and reviewers who signed up to help promote the release of Cruel Promise, I am so sorry I was unable to get ARCs out to you sooner. But I hope their story was worth the wait.

And to my readers, thank you so much for all of your incredible love and support and for following me on this amazing journey of love, social justice, and happily ever afters.

ABOUT THE AUTHOR

Daniela Romero is a USA Today and Wall Street Journal bestselling author. She enjoys writing steamy, new-adult and paranormal romance that delivers an emotional roller coaster sure to take your breath away.

Her books feature a diverse cast of characters with rich and vibrant cultures in an effort to effectively portray the world we all live in. One that is so beautifully colorful.

Daniela is a Bay Area native though she currently lives in Washington State with her sarcastic husband and their three tiny terrors.

In her free time, Daniela enjoys frequent naps, binge reading her favorite romance books, and is known to crochet while watching television because her ADHD brain can never do just one thing at a time.

Stop by her website to find all the fun and unique ways you can stalk her. And while you're there you can check out some free bonus scenes from your favorite books, learn about her Patreon, order signed copies of her books, and swoon over her gorgeous alternative cover editions.

www.daniela-romero.com

You can join my newsletter by visiting
https://hi.switchy.io/VIP

Made in the USA
Middletown, DE
17 August 2023

36913334R00183